Building Billions - Part 2

Building Billions, Volume 2

Lexy Timms

Published by Dark Shadow Publishing, 2018.

This is a work of fiction. Similarities to real people, places, or events are entirely coincidental.

BUILDING BILLIONS - PART 2

First edition. April 5, 2018.

Copyright © 2018 Lexy Timms.

Written by Lexy Timms.

Also by Lexy Timms

A Chance at Forever Series
Forever Perfect
Forever Desired
Forever Together

Alpha Bad Boy Motorcycle Club Triology
Alpha Biker
Alpha Revenge
Alpha Outlaw
Alpha Purpose

BBW Romance Series
Capturing Her Beauty
Pursuing Her Dreams
Tracing Her Curves

Beating the Biker Series
Making Her His

Making the Break
Making of Them

Billionaire Holiday Romance Series
Driving Home for Christmas
The Valentine Getaway
Cruising Love

Billionaire in Disguise Series
Facade
Illusion
Charade

Billionaire Secrets Series
The Secret
Freedom
Courage

Building Billions
Building Billions - Part 1
Building Billions - Part 2

Conquering Warrior Series
Ruthless

Diamond in the Rough Anthology
Billionaire Rock
Billionaire Rock - part 2

Dominating PA Series
Her Personal Assistant - Part 1
Her Personal Assistant Box Set

Fake Billionaire Series
Faking It
Temporary CEO
Caught in the Act
Never Tell A Lie
Fake Christmas

Firehouse Romance Series
Caught in Flames
Burning With Desire
Craving the Heat
Firehouse Romance Complete Collection

Fortune Riders MC Series
Billionaire Biker
Billionaire Ransom

Billionaire Misery

Fragile Series
Fragile Touch
Fragile Kiss
Fragile Love

Hades' Spawn Motorcycle Club
One You Can't Forget
One That Got Away
One That Came Back
One You Never Leave
One Christmas Night
Hades' Spawn MC Complete Series

Heart of Stone Series
The Protector
The Guardian
The Warrior

Heart of the Battle Series
Celtic Viking
Celtic Rune
Celtic Mann
Heart of the Battle Series Box Set

Heistdom Series
Master Thief

Just About Series
About Love
About Truth
About Forever

Love You Series
Love Life
Need Love
My Love

Managing the Bosses Series
The Boss
The Boss Too
Who's the Boss Now
Love the Boss
I Do the Boss
Wife to the Boss
Employed by the Boss
Brother to the Boss
Senior Advisor to the Boss
Forever the Boss
Gift for the Boss - Novella 3.5
Christmas With the Boss

Moment in Time
Highlander's Bride
Victorian Bride
Modern Day Bride
A Royal Bride
Forever the Bride

Outside the Octagon
Submit

Reverse Harem Series
Primals

RIP Series
Track the Ripper
Hunt the Ripper
Pursue the Ripper

R&S Rich and Single Series
Alex Reid
Parker

Saving Forever

Saving Forever - Part 1
Saving Forever - Part 2
Saving Forever - Part 3
Saving Forever - Part 4
Saving Forever - Part 5
Saving Forever - Part 6
Saving Forever Part 7
Saving Forever - Part 8
Saving Forever Boxset Books #1-3

Southern Romance Series
Little Love Affair
Siege of the Heart
Freedom Forever
Soldier's Fortune

Tattooist Series
Confession of a Tattooist
Surrender of a Tattooist
Heart of a Tattooist
Hopes & Dreams of a Tattooist

Tennessee Romance
Whisky Lullaby
Whisky Melody
Whisky Harmony

The Brush Of Love Series
Every Night
Every Day
Every Time
Every Way
Every Touch

The Debt
The Debt: Part 1 - Damn Horse
The Debt: Complete Collection

The University of Gatica Series
The Recruiting Trip
Faster
Higher
Stronger
Dominate
No Rush
University of Gatica - The Complete Series

T.N.T. Series
Troubled Nate Thomas - Part 1
Troubled Nate Thomas - Part 2
Troubled Nate Thomas - Part 3

Undercover Series
Perfect For Me
Perfect For You
Perfect For Us

Unknown Identity Series
Unknown
Unpublished
Unexposed
Unsure
Unwritten
Unknown Identity Box Set: Books #1-3

Unlucky Series
Unlucky in Love
UnWanted
UnLoved Forever

Standalone
Wash
Loving Charity
Summer Lovin'
Love & College
Billionaire Heart
First Love
Frisky and Fun Romance Box Collection

Managing the Bosses Box Set #1-3

Building Billions
Part #2
By Lexy Timms
Copyright 2018

ALL RIGHTS RESERVED. No part of this publication may be reproduced, stored in or introduced into a retrieval system, or transmitted, in any form, or by any means (electronic, mechanical, photocopying, recording, or otherwise) without the prior written permission of both the copyright owner and the above publisher of this book.

This is a work of fiction. Names, characters, places, brands, media, and incidents are either the product of the author's imagination or are used fictitiously. Any resemblance to an actual person, living or dead, events, or locales is entirely coincidental. The author acknowledges the trademarked status and trademark owners of various products referenced in this work of fiction, which have been used without permission. The publication/use of these trademarks is not authorized, associated with, or sponsored by the trademark owners.

All rights reserved.
Freedom
Building Billions Part #2
Copyright 2018 by Lexy Timms
Cover by: Book Cover by Design[1]

---

1. http://bookcoverbydesign.co.uk/

Building Billions

Part 1
Part 2
Part 3

Find Lexy Timms:

LEXY TIMMS NEWSLETTER:
http://eepurl.com/9i0vD
Lexy Timms Facebook Page:
https://www.facebook.com/SavingForever
Lexy Timms Website:
http://www.lexytimms.com

Want to read more...
For **FREE?**

Sign up for Lexy Timms' newsletter
And she'll send you
A paid read, for FREE!
Sign up for news and updates!
http://eepurl.com/9i0vD

Building Billions Part 2 Blurb

BY USA TODAY BESTSELLING Author, Lexy Timms.
It was only supposed to be one night.

Except making out with your boss when his girlfriend walks into his office, doesn't sound as innocent as it seems.

Maybe Jimmy's ex-girlfriend has a bit of a grudge against them. Maybe running into them a week later out together only fuels the fire and her determination to take them down. And if not them, at least Jimmy's company.

For Ashley, focusing on work is a lot better than looking at social media. She's good with numbers—it's her thing—and when she can't figure out why the numbers aren't lining up for the company, she starts investigating.

When the truth comes out, Jimmy doesn't believe her.

How much are you willing to risk for the one you love?

Like the hit song, **LOVE HURTS.**

Chapter 1

Jimmy
(One Week Later)

Big Steps was on the up and up, and it seemed my wedding ring was doing wonders. Men no longer questioned whether I was a commitment man during a dinner meeting or in an investor meeting. No one was asking me who I'd married as of yet—probably assuming—and I never offered the information out.

Except I knew what my actual lucky charm was. I could blame it on the ring all I wanted to, but having Ashley officially at my side was the best thing that could've happened to me. To my company too.

We'd been seeing each other officially for an entire week. And while having her around was doing wonders for my disposition, it did make work an exercise in restraint. Looking up and seeing her office right there was hard. There were moments when I imagined striding into her space, locking the door, and having my way with her on top of her desk with the sun sinking below the skyline and her beautiful skin lit up with the decadent colors of the sunset.

She was a distraction of the best kind.

I looked up and saw her head down, furiously jotting down something. Numbers or equations. Possibly notes. She'd had her meeting with Mr. Matthews that I had sat in on, and she'd handled herself with a poise any woman would've been envious of. She was gentle but firm in her talking points. Mr. Matthews either needed to commit to a quarterly donation like the rest of the investors or there would have to be a fee that was enacted every time one of his checks failed to clear. Ashley clearly outlined all the heartache his pending checks put us through and the fees that came along with dipping into accounts we shouldn't be drawing from.

She was direct with her numbers, great with her eye contact, and just gentle enough to wear down Mr. Matthews' walls. Not only did she get him to commit to a quarterly investment, she also got him to commit to a minimum quarterly investment that was ten thousand dollars more than he was paying originally.

The woman had no idea what she was capable of.

"Miss Ternbeau?"

I watched Ashley look up at me as she held her office phone to her ear.

"Yes, Mr. Sheldon?"

"Could you come into my office at your earliest convenience? I've got some things I want to pass your way."

"I'll be there as soon as I can," she said.

I watched her put her phone down as she grinned and shook her head. She finished up what she was doing while I leaned back in my chair and watched her. I loved it when her red hair piled in her face. Hell, I loved it when she wore it down in general. She was doing more of that now. She still wore a hair tie around her wrist, but for the past week, she had worn her hair down.

And part of me was convinced it was specifically for me.

"You wanted to see me?" Ashley asked.

"Close my door, please. This meeting is private," I said.

She turned around and closed the door as I got up and strode over to her.

"So, what's this super-secret—?"

I muffled her sentiment with a kiss. My hand pressed into the small of her back as her hands smoothed up my chest. I closed my eyes and felt her fist my coat. That small little action proved to me she wanted my body closer. I pressed her quietly against my closed office door, my hand snaking down her ass and cupping just the slightest handful.

But when I opened my eyes and broke the kiss, she had an almost pained look on her face.

"Are you all right?" I asked.

"Did you call me into your office simply to kiss me?" Ashley asked.

"And if I did?"

"Not complaining. Just ..."

"I didn't call you in here only to kiss you," I said. "I also wanted to ask you to dinner tonight."

"Is that an offer? Or merely a statement of the offer you were going to offer?"

"You're lucky I had my coffee this morning. I actually followed that statement."

Her smile lit a fire in my chest as my hand slid from her ass to her hair. I ran my fingers through it, studying the way it framed her face. I ran my thumb along her blushing cheek, her eyes fluttering closed as she took in my touch.

"Have dinner with me tonight, Ashley."

"I'd love to have dinner with you," she said.

But there was still that look in her eye, and I wanted to know why it was there.

"What's going through your mind?" I asked.

"That's the first time we've kissed in your office since ... you know. Everything."

"You can say her name. She isn't Voldemort."

"But she's dangerous. Don't you see that?" she asked.

"Nina isn't dangerous. Merely upset."

"She told you she was going to make you pay, and she seemed like she meant it."

"And I'm sure during that moment, she did mean it. But Nina is a woman who doesn't understand how to operate without someone feeding her cash. She bit the hand nourishing her, and she got burned. It happens to the best of us."

"I still don't quite understand how your arrangement with her worked," she said.

"It was simple. She needed debts paid off, and I needed a woman to come whenever I called to attend charity functions and social events. I took care of her need, and she took care of mine."

"Yeah. You don't realize how weird that sounds, do you?"

"I understand exactly how weird it sounds. But now, I have you. And that's all I want to focus on," I said.

"I'm still worried. I'm a woman, Jimmy."

"And a fine woman at that," I said with a grin.

"I know how a woman's mind works. If she really wants to do something to you, she'll find a way."

"You shouldn't worry about her. Nina's trying to start things, trying to rift us apart so she can swoop back in and try to wrangle my wallet out of my pocket again. Knowing her, within the month, she'll have no way to pay for the lavish lifestyle I afforded her. This is all about money. She has no more strings left to tug on."

"Jimmy, I don't—"

I silenced her with another kiss and felt her melt into me. Her arms slipped around my neck, and her fingers curled into the bottom tendrils of my hair. Her touch sent shivers down my spine. Her tongue felt like velvet against the inside of my cheek. She cradled into me effortlessly, tugging at dark parts of me I wanted to indulge.

Like we had that night.

"I'm looking forward to dinner," Ashley said as she broke the kiss.

"I'll pick you up at your place," I said.

"I can meet you there. It's fine."

"Ashley, let me pick you up for our date tonight."

"I'm not going to be there much longer anyway. I'm moving in a couple of weeks."

"Congratulations. Where to?" I asked.

"Ocean Homes."

"That's a very nice place and hard to get into. Congratulations."

"You already said that."

"But I'm picking you up tonight," I said.

"Jimmy."

"No. Ashley, I want to take you out to dinner, which means I want to pick you up. I don't care where you live now or where you're about to live. I want to pick you up, drive you to dinner, pay for dinner, and then drop you off. Is that okay?"

I watched her sigh as she shook her head and smiled.

"Fine. Okay. I'll see you around eight?"

"Perfect. See you then."

The rest of the day moved at a snail's pace. Focusing was hard, but I knew there was a prize for me at the end of the tunnel. If I could get everything done, I could change in my office, leave to get Ashley, and not have to worry about the work that would follow me into the weekend. I listened as the rest of the office building dumped out onto the busy streets of Miami, the lights of the hallway dimming to a dull roar. I typed up all the information I needed into the system and double-checked my schedule, making sure everything was right before I carried the paperwork to Ross's office.

Then, it was time for me to get changed.

I pulled Ashley's home address from her professional file, and I figured out why she didn't want me picking her up. She lived in a very run-down part of Miami. Had I known that earlier, I would've called whoever I needed to call to have her moved out right away. She was in a very dangerous part of town, and as a single woman, it wasn't good for her to be living there, much less walking to and from her car by herself. I raced down the elevator, hopped into my Bugatti, and whipped in and out of traffic to get to her.

I pulled up to her apartment complex, and she was standing outside waiting for me like she didn't understand the unsavory people who trekked in and out of this part of the city. I got out of my car hell-bent on convincing her to move immediately, but her outfit stopped me in my tracks. Her curves were covered in a dark purple dress. It fell off her shoulders and framed her luscious breasts perfectly. It clung to her waist before dripping into a skirt that was higher in the front than it was in the back.

And her heels. The dark purple heels flexed her legs and showed off her toned calves.

She was breathtaking, and I forgot all about the rehearsed speech in my head.

"Hey, Jimmy."

Her soft voice ripped me from my trance as I held my hand out to take hers. I brought it my lips to kiss and led her around the car. I helped her dip down into her seat and then quickly strode around to get us the hell out of the place.

The smile that crossed her face as my car raced into the distance tingled my skin.

"So, where are we going?" Ashley asked.

"Somewhere fit for that beautiful dress you're wearing," I said.

I looked over and saw her blush as a small giggle fell from her lips.

"You look incredible, Ashley."

"That suit looks mighty fine on you, too, Jimmy."

"We're going to Joe's Stone Crab. It's an excellent place for seafood, and they've got live music playing tonight."

"Oh, dancing. I haven't danced since—"

My eyebrow quirked as I looked over at her. I saw her pressing her thighs together as she cut off her sentiment. I knew what she was about to say. She hadn't danced since the night of the party, the night her body had opened itself up to me and introduced me to a world no other woman had ripped me into.

I turned my eyes back to the road as my hand snaked over to hers.

We walked into the restaurant, and the band was already playing. We put in our order for food and drink, and then I held out my hand for Ashley. She took it lovingly, her delicate hand seated in the palm of mine.

I twirled her out onto the floor and carried her around.

We danced and laughed. I twirled her out and spun her back in. I bent down and picked her up, hoisting her into the air before catching her against my body. I dipped her back and smiled at her, watching the way her beautiful eyes lit up.

I had no idea why this woman brought such a joy into my life, but I was determined to keep it as long as possible.

I brought her back upright and pulled her close to my body. The music slowed down, and the lights dimmed a bit, our bodies swaying to the music. Her hand was cradled in mine, and my arm was wrapped around her lower back. She swayed with me, bowing into me with the slightest curve as her body molded to mine.

"I never thought I'd have such a good time with a man without constant conversation," Ashley said.

"Sometimes, people don't need to talk to enjoy the presence of one another," I said.

"Good thing. I'm sure she doesn't have much to talk about."

That grating voice caused me to clench my jaw. I flung my gaze over to the woman standing beside us as Ashley's jaw dropped in shock. There she was, the bane of my fucking existence with those harsh gray eyes and that straight black hair that hung like a trap waiting to catch any rich man who came her way so she could sink her claws into him.

Nina.

With some friend of hers that kept eyeing Ashley with a disgusted look on her face.

"Nina," I said.

"Jimmy. Shouldn't shock me you're out with your latest pet."

I felt Ashley tense in my arms as I pulled her closer to my side.

"Is that what you felt like?" I asked. "A pet? This is Ashley, my new Account Representative for my investors."

"I guess people can still screw their way to the top," Nina's friend said.

I felt Ashley shudder as my eyes gazed down at her. I could see her eyes filling with tears, despite her want to hold them back. Her cheeks were reddening, and the smile on Nina's face was growing.

She was liking this.

She was getting a kick out of insulting Ashley.

"Mr. Sheldon, is something wrong?"

I turned my eyes to the manager as Ashley stepped away from my grasp.

"It seems you'll let anyone in here nowadays," I said as I looked at Nina and her friend. "I would enjoy our food to-go and a bottle of your finest wine. Let our waitress know I'll leave a decent tip on her table for the trouble I've caused her."

"I'll get right on it and let her know," the manager said.

Then, I watched him escort the two women away from us.

I took Ashley back in my arms, trying to calm her as people started rushing around. There was no need for them to rush. The bulk of the problem had been dispelled. I could feel Ashley trembling in her effort to conceal her emotions from the public, but that was something I liked about her.

She didn't try to fake her emotional disposition.

"Here is your food and your check, Mr. Sheldon," the waitress says. "And the bottle of wine is on us. For the trouble our patron and her friend caused you."

"Tell the general manager he's a miracle worker. And thank you for your hard work and patience," I said.

I paid for the food and left the woman an outstanding tip. I took Ashley's hand and led her from the restaurant, our bags hanging from my wrist. I walked Ashley to her side of the car to help her in and put the food in the trunk before dipping into my car.

"Before you say anything, you still have nothing to worry about," I said.

"I don't know how you're going to convince me this time that we don't," she said.

"It was a coincidence that Nina ran into us here. There's a good chance she was with her friend because she couldn't afford it herself. They're nothing, okay? They're a product of the money they can swindle from friends and family. They can't hold their own in society. In a regular job. In a company like mine. Not like you can. They use their looks to get what they want. But you have intelligence."

"You saying I'm not a looker, Mr. Sheldon?"

Her cheeky grin tugged at my gut as I leaned in close to her lips.

"I'm saying you have substance, and that makes every curve of your body that much more desirable."

We shared a kiss in my car as her hand came up to cup my cheek. Her touch was tender and loving, full of kindness and a steady strength. Our tongues lapped against one another's calmly, stoking a fire that burst in my toes. I reluctantly pulled back from her as my stomach began to growl. The food in the back seat was beginning to permeate my car, and I was hungry.

"Fancy a dinner underneath the stars?" I asked.

I drove us out to an abandoned park and worked my way into the middle of a meadow. I rolled back the sunroof before I got out to get the food, and then we scooted our chairs back and enjoyed a silent dinner. Once in a while, Ashley would chime in with something about a constellation she saw, a backstory or a fact about it that would broaden my knowledge about her. It was like she was a walking encyclopedia, devouring everything she could get her hands on and still thirsting for more knowledge.

I loved that in a person. It was an honorable trait, to want to always know more.

But the dinner was over too soon, and it was time to take her back.

We pulled up to her apartment complex, and I cringed at the sight of it, dark and dreary with the outside crumbling away. How long had she been living in a place like this? Why in the world wasn't she somewhere nicer? A hundred more dollars a month and she could've gotten a small place for herself on the other side of town.

Not as glamorous as Ocean Homes but much safer than this place.

We stood in front of her apartment door for a long time before I watched her hand settle on the doorknob.

"Aren't you going to invite me in?" I asked coyly.

"I'm actually kind of tired," Ashley said.

"But we have a bottle of wine to open."

"I'm sorry. It's just been a long day. And a long night."

"Did you not enjoy yourself?" I asked.

"I did. But it doesn't change the fact that it's past ten o'clock, and I'm secretly an old woman."

"You sure are limber on the dance floor for an old woman."

"I'm sorry, Jimmy."

"No need to be sorry, but I want you to take this bottle of wine. It's a very nice vintage, and when you move into your new place, you and your friend can celebrate."

"Cass?" she asked.

"I remember you mentioning a wine and pizza night with someone. Figured I could provide the wine for your next one."

"Even though I know you didn't buy this for that reason, thank you," she said with a grin.

I dipped down to kiss her on the cheek and watched her walk back into her apartment. I heaved a heavy sigh and then made my way back down to my car. I hated leaving her in a place like this, leaving her to fend for herself with people staring at us like they were. But she was an independent woman, and I wasn't going to try and stifle that simply because I thought she deserved more.

Better.

Grander.

I slipped into my car and started it up. I closed my eyes and gathered myself, trying to shake the desire to rush up those steps and force myself into her apartment.

Then as I flipped the car into reverse, a light tapping sounded on my window.

I looked over and saw Ashley's beautiful, round eyes reflecting the same constellations she'd rattled on about over the course of our meadow-laden dinner.

"Yes?" I asked as I rolled down my window.

"Maybe just a nightcap?" she asked.

I threw the car into park faster than she could lean up from my car. I offered my arm to her, and she smiled, slipping her skin against my suit. Her warmth comforted me as I led her up the stairs, and then the two of us entered her apartment.

I tried not to stare too much at the water-stained ceiling or the kitchen appliances that were fit for no place other than a junkyard.

"I still don't think it's a good idea for you to stay the night," Ashley said. "So only a small nightcap."

I reached my arm out for her body and pulled her flush against mine.

"Whatever makes you comfortable," I said.

I dipped my lips to her neck and pressed a kiss to her pulse point. I felt her sigh against me, her breath heating my skin. Her hands gripped my suit coat, pulling me closer as my lips nibbled at her exposed shoulders.

I had a plan for this woman tonight.

I was going to treat her to something I knew she deserved.

"Do you want the wine o-or—"

I moved my lips to her tender breasts, biting into them as she moaned.

"Or what?" I asked.

"Jimmy," she said in a whisper.

Her hands flew to my hair, and my hands gripped her ass. I picked her up and walked her back into the only other room she had in her small, dank apartment. I settled her on her bed, being careful of the moving boxes she had already packed.

Then, I settled my body between her legs.

I could see her nipples poking through the fabric of her gorgeous dress. I kissed up her thigh, my tongue flicking and my lips nibbling. She flinched at every move as she spread herself for me, her hands running through her hair and massaging her own breasts. She was a vision with her legs spread and her heels digging into her mattress and her skin flush with desire. I mouthed over her cotton panties, the fabric darkened with her arousal.

Her scent was intoxicating, and I knew this was the drink I wanted.

This was the nightcap I wanted her to offer me.

I slid her panties to the side and dipped my tongue between her folds. They were succulent and juicy, dripping with fluids that poured effortlessly onto my tongue. Decadent sighs fell from her lips as her body jolted, jerking with every flick I delivered to her clit.

I sucked, and I rolled and pressed deeply into her. I could feel her shaking as she propped her legs on my shoulders. I bent her legs forward, rendering her immobile as my tongue devoured her, licking up everything she had to give me as her hands tangled in my hair.

"Jimmy. Yes. Oh my gosh. I'm ... it's—oh!"

Her chest arched into me as my tongue flattened out over her clit. I felt her arousal pooling against my chin, then gathering and dripping down my neck. I held onto her trembling body as she contracted against me, her hands tightening against my scalp.

She dropped to the bed and panted for air, her skin flushed red and her legs weakly trembling.

"That didn't take long," I said with a grin.

But there was a part of me that was disappointed in that fact.

"Then you must be really good at what you do," Ashley said breathlessly.

"We'll just have to work on your tolerance."

I gathered her juices from my chin and held it up to her lips. She parted that luscious pout I loved to kiss and sucked my finger in, licking herself off me. I groaned, feeling my cock twitch behind my pants.

But this wasn't about me tonight.

This was about her and convincing her she had nothing to worry about while she was at my side.

"Tastes better than I thought it would," she said.

"You little minx," I said.

"Would you like to lie down next to me for a bit? I can imagine that must have tired you out."

I hovered over her, my body blanketing hers as her hands traced my collar. I wanted to. Oh, how I wanted to sink down next to her, but I knew she was in a post-orgasmic haze. The only words I could trust right now where the ones she'd told me before I'd thrown her over the edge into the ecstasy bubbling behind her gaze.

"I promised you I wouldn't stay, and I'm going to keep that promise," I said.

"Then I take it back. No more promise," she said.

"I respect you," I said. "I want you to know that."

"I know. I do."

"And I don't want to squash my chances at scoring again."

She giggled as I winked at her, and she playfully slapped my chest. I wrapped my hand around hers and brought it to my lips, kissing her skin one last time. Our eyes connected, and I felt a peace overcome my body, blanketing me with a happiness I'd never felt before.

This woman affected me in ways I'd never understand.

"Here, let me walk you to the door," Ashley said.

"Why don't I take your heels off and you settle into bed?" I asked.

"Sleep? In this dress? Do you know how much this thing cost me?"

"I'll reimburse you," I said with a grin.

"Let me walk you to the door, Jimmy. Come on. Help me up."

I pulled her up to her feet, and she wobbled for a second. I caught her in my arms, and the blush that ran across her cheeks was delightful. I buried my smile as she took my hand, but after that, she fell quiet. She walked me to the door with a somber look on her face and kissed my cheek before she opened it.

"Drive safely, okay?" she asked.

"Always," I said.

I waited for her to say something else, but it never came. I dipped to her cheek to kiss her one last time, and then I stepped out into the nighttime. The door closed quietly behind me, and I turned back, waiting to see if she would come after me one last time.

Then, I made my way back to my car and headed home.

Chapter 2

Ashley

"Jimmy's right. You shouldn't worry about that stuck up bitch."

"Cass. Good hell, could you have said that any louder?" I asked.

"Possibly. Want me to try?" she asked.

"No, but thanks for the offer?"

"Look, what Nina did at dinner was wrong, but Jimmy handled it well. Very well, actually. Ash, he kicked some dumbass women out of a restaurant for you. Then took you for a dinner in the park. Underneath the stars. You didn't talk his ear off about them, did you?"

"I may have told him a few things," I said.

"Ugh. Ashley. No man wants to hear about the backstory of the constellation Andromeda."

"Well, he enjoyed it enough to come up to my apartment afterward," I said with a smile.

"You didn't," she said.

"Not all the way. But he did enjoy himself on my body a bit."

"You didn't!"

"Cass, it was so good. He was so good."

"Did he stay? Please tell me he stayed."

"I wanted him to afterward, but before that, I told him it probably wasn't a good idea. He stuck with that notion instead of giving into what I said afterward."

"So, he's polite, rich, good in bed, and a gentleman? Does he have a brother?" she asked.

"You're so bad," I said.

"And apparently you're not far behind."

It was nice to get coffee with Cassidy before work. We'd made it a thing now that I could afford to splurge on morning coffee. Especially since I'd spilled the beans that Jimmy and I were now apparently a "thing." Which I didn't mind, but I was still worried about Nina. I was concerned about her wiggling her way into whatever relationship we were trying to figure out because of her prior relationship with him. When money was involved, people always got desperate.

There were many times where I would've done almost anything to get a few more bucks in my pocket.

"You're worrying again. I see it on your face," Cass said.

"I know you guys are right, and I hear you, but I'm still worried about Nina," I said.

"Don't let it ruin your chances with Jimmy, that's all I'm asking. You're happier than I've seen you in a long time. Don't let this stupid woman ruin it for you."

"I'll try not to," I said.

I hugged Cass's neck before the two of us parted ways for work. My mind kept going back to last night, how good his tongue was and how wonderful his kiss had felt on my bare skin. I enjoyed his touch, and I enjoyed his body against mine, but that taste of him wasn't nearly enough. My body was still riding that high, and my nipples kept puckering at the most inopportune moments.

I wouldn't have complained one bit if Jimmy had taken me right there in my bedroom last night.

I walked by Jimmy's office, trying to ready myself for the day. I peeked in and saw he wasn't there and felt a bubble of disappointment roll my gut. Was everything okay? He was usually in his office by now. I fumbled with my office keys, opened my door, turned the light on, and sighed.

The view from my office was gorgeous, and I'd never get used to it greeting me.

"Good morning."

I jumped at the sound of Jimmy's voice, and I almost dropped my coffee. The two of us shared a laugh as he picked my purse up off the floor. Then he came in and shut my door. I walked over to set my coffee down and reclined on the edge of my desk.

"The power stance. It looks good on you," he said.

"Figured I'd give it a try. It's not very often you come into my office," I said.

"I wanted to make sure you were okay. You know, from last night."

"I'm wonderful," I said. "But thank you for asking."

"Good," he said as he walked to me. "That's good to hear."

He was standing in front of me, toe to toe as his eyes held mine. I felt the heat rising in the room and the desire for him tugging at my gut. My nipples were already standing at attention behind my bra, and I could feel my knees growing weak.

Just one kiss.

That was all I needed.

I grabbed his suit coat and pulled him into me, crashing our lips together. I wanted him. Desperately. I wanted him to wipe everything off my desk and take me right there on it. His hands fell to my hips as my legs spread for him, his body stepping between them as he towered over my form. His hand came up to cup my cheek, our lips releasing before our forehead connected.

We were heaving, breathing one another's air as our eyes stayed closed.

I felt his grasp on me as I looked down. I saw his pants tented, the indentation of his thick cock pressed against the fabric. I moaned at the sight as Jimmy kissed my ear, trailing his lips down my neck and nipping at my skin.

I felt him leaning me back onto my desk as my legs wrapped around him.

"I can't stop thinking about last night," Jimmy said.

"I wished I could've had more of you," I said breathlessly.

"I could lock the office door, press you against the windows, and show you off to the world as they walk by unaware of the beauty above them."

I whimpered at his words as his hand teased my breasts. He ran his finger along where he knew my nipple would be, and I jumped. I felt his cock pulse against my thigh. My head was spinning, and my mind was at a standstill.

But the sound of heels walking to my office cut the moment short.

Jimmy pulled himself away and stuffed his hand down his pants. He rearranged himself as I fixed my clothing. The heels continued to walk by as we held our breath, and then we started laughing as they receded down the hallway.

"Not a good idea, is it?" I asked.

"Maybe not now," Jimmy said. "But at eight in the evening when everyone's gone? Possibly."

The darkness in his eyes heated my core as I bit down on my lower lip. I had to get work done. I had to get focused and ready for the day. Jimmy bent down and placed a kiss on my neck, causing my eyes to roll back as he grinned.

"Have a good day, Miss Ternbeau."

Then in a flash, he was gone.

I flopped down into my chair and tried to focus on what I was doing. I pulled up some balance sheets from earlier, a favor I was doing for the accounting department. They hadn't found a replacement for me yet, and removing me meant they were swamped. Since the investor's accounts were all settled for now, I had the time to do them a solid.

Especially since it gave me leverage over Mr. Brent.

I looked back over the numbers and noticed some irregularities. I'd made notes about them yesterday, but I wanted to triple-check and make sure I was right. One look became two, and two became three, and by the time lunch rolled around, I was knee-deep in numbers that weren't right and not even halfway finished with my other responsibilities. I kept calculating numbers and highlighting things, making notes in the margins of the papers I'd printed out in my office.

Something was wrong, just like those balance sheets from before. At first, I thought it could have been the algorithm being used, a wrong number or symbol in the equation itself. After looking over the numbers yet again, though, I wasn't so sure anymore.

"Ashley?"

"Yes, Jimmy?"

"You wanna take a break for lunch?"

I sighed as I lifted my head, my mind racing with questions I needed answers to.

"I can't," I said. "I've got a lot to get done here."

"Want me to send you something up then? I could sit at your desk and eat while you work," he said.

"That's very kind of you, but I really need to focus."

"I'll send something up for you to munch on anyway. Sans my presence. Don't work yourself too hard, though. And take a break at some point in time."

"Will do. Promise."

I didn't feel I could bring up the irregularities to him yet. I wasn't sure why they were occurring, and it could be a malfunction in the tech somewhere, which meant it was a job for IT, not accounting.

My door opened, and I smelled a beautiful plate of noodles heading in my direction. I looked up and saw Jimmy standing there, a tray of vegetable lo mein in his hand. I sighed and cocked my head, giggling as I shook my head.

"Sans your presence?" I asked.

"I'm just the delivery boy today," Jimmy said. "Nothing else."

"Delivery boy. That could get fun."

I watched his eyes light up as he made his way to my desk.

I shuffled the balance sheets out of view so he wouldn't see what I was doing. If there was something wrong, I wanted all the answers before I went to him. That was my job, after all, bringing him issues as well as probable solutions.

That and he would probably get upset with Mr. Brent again.

"I will need you in some meetings this afternoon, so make sure you're in my office by two."

"Is there an investor's meeting I forgot about?" I asked.

"No, but the yearly budget meetings are coming up. I'd like you to jot down the numbers and take notes. You know, things that'll help us figure out what the coming budgets for the departments should be."

"I'll be there," I said with a smile.

He set my food down and eyed me before he left the office. He knew something was up. He knew something was amiss, but since he wasn't pressing it, that meant he trusted me with it. I looked at the clock and saw it was almost one in the afternoon, so I grabbed the noodles and began eating them. I kept taking notes and running numbers as I mindlessly ate, finding more and more problems the further I dug into the balance sheets.

What in the world was going on?

Chapter 3

Jimmy

"Jimmy Sheldon."

"You still not introducing yourself as 'James'? Makes you sound like a teenage boy."

"Markus?" I asked.

"The hell else would it be?"

"Holy shit. Markus. How in the world have you been?"

"I'm coming into town to check up on some things. You free?" Markus asked.

"Of course, I'm free. And it's about damn time you came back into town. What's it been, a year?"

"Little over that. I'm flying in on Friday and staying for a couple of weeks. I've got some business to handle that requires my face."

"Who screwed up now?" I asked.

"You don't wanna know. But I'll fill you in over dinner when I get into town."

"Can't wait to hear what you're gonna do to the poor soul. You always have the most creative solutions besides simply firing someone."

"Firing people leaves you with a hole to fill. Makes more work for the businessman. But teach them a lesson they'll never forget? Less work, more entertainment."

"Sounds like the ruthless man I know," I said. "You really need to get back to your biannual trips out here. Miami misses you."

"I know, I know. Business has been up, and it's chained me to my damn desk. When do you wanna get dinner?"

"Anytime you're free," I said. "And multiple times, if possible."

"You got it. You're the only person I can tolerate in Miami anyway. Which reminds me. Leave Nina at home."

"Then you're in luck. I broke up with Nina about a week ago."

"Thank fuck. Do I have Ross to thank for that?" he asked.

"A bit, yes, but it was time for her to go. I had another woman who deserved my time anyway. She's great. You'd love her."

"That was quick. But then that's always been your specialty."

"Working quick or tearing through women?" I asked.

The two of us shared a laugh as I leaned back in my office chair.

"Her name's Ashley. She's our Account Representative for the investors."

"Ah, dating a bit of corporate. Be careful with that. If things go south, I've seen companies go under for less."

"We're taking it slow. Ish."

"Uh-huh. And how long did you two start this ... thing after you ended it with Nina?"

"Two days?"

"Right. Keep your wits about you. Pussy mesmerizes the best of us."

"You know Nina and my relationship wasn't traditional."

"Boy, I'm well aware of that. Pulled a similar stunt before I ended up marrying the woman to save face to the public. It's common for businessmen to do that, but I'm glad you got rid of her. I would've hated to see you make the mistake I did. I swear to fuck, I married Satan's bride."

"Call me the second you're in town. If you're not too jet-lagged, we'll get some drinks. On me."

"Hell, yeah, on you. I'll be too jet-lagged to reach for my wallet," he said.

"Talk to you soon, Markus."

"Yep."

I was beyond excited for Markus coming into town. I went by Ashley's office at the end of the day and offered to take her out to dinner. She looked back at me with that beautiful smile and quickly closed her office down, and then the two of us headed to my car. We went to this quaint little restaurant on the corner and had a bite to eat, and I could feel the heat radiating from her body. Her feet kept sliding close to mine underneath the table, and I felt my neck blushing with lust for her.

Now that I knew what she tasted like, I wanted more of her.

"Wanna head back to my place?" I asked.

"Sure. I think it's about time I see what you call home," Ashley said.

"You'll never guess who called me today."

"Who?" she asked.

"Markus Bryant," I said.

"Wait, one of our investors called you? Did I do something wrong?"

"No, no, no. It's nothing like that. Markus isn't simply any investor. He was the first investor I ever took on. It was his mentorship and guidance that shot Big Steps up the ladder as quickly as we got there. He only comes into town once or twice a year to check on things, but it's always a good time when he arrives."

"Wow. That sounds like a very important person in your life," she said.

"He is. It's been over a year since he's been in Miami, and I can't wait for him to get here."

"You guys gonna go do all sorts of guy stuff? Like fish and hunt and stuff dead animal heads and mount them in your office?"

"Is that what you picture Ross and me doing whenever we go out?"

"Nope. You and Ross are men who play squash in those tight shorty-shorts with those loud grunts."

"You imagine Ross in tight shorty-shorts?" I asked.

"Isn't that what men wear to play squash?"

"I don't know. I don't play squash."

We pulled into the parking garage of my place, and I led her up to my penthouse apartment. It was my second favorite place to be, especially now that Nina was no longer tainting it with her presence. I pressed my hand into the small of Ashley's back as I guided her into my home. Her eyes took in the expanse of everything before her eyes fell on the view from my windows.

"Floor-to-ceiling windows must be your trademark aesthetic," she said.

"I do like a good view," I said.

Her eyes looked up at me as she blushed, but I could tell there was something wrong.

Still.

"What is it?" I asked.

"What's what?"

"What's bothering you, Ashley?"

I watched her face grow somber as she cast her gaze back out the windows.

"It's Nina. All this ... stuff with her. But I promise to put my worries to the side. I know I can't dwell on it forever."

"I promise you really have nothing to worry about with her," I said.

"I've always been a worrier. It's written in my DNA."

"Then I'll do everything I can to settle you down," I said.

My hands fell onto her upper arms, massaging them as a small sigh escaped her lips. I moved to her shoulders, massaging the tension from them as the sun finally set below the skyline. Darkness covered my apartment as Ashley's curvy silhouette pressed into my body, into my warmth, into my touch.

I wanted to give her some kind of distraction, something to rid her mind of the worries rattling around in her head. I worked my thumbs up her neck as her head tilted forward, offering me all the access in the world.

Then, I tilted her head to the side and turned her lips to mine.

"You look beautiful tonight," I said.

She responded by grasping the tie around my neck.

Chapter 4

Ashley

I grabbed his tie and crashed our lips together. I'd wanted him for so long, and now I finally had him. I could feel how badly he wanted me. How quickly he pinned my body to the glass of his window. His chiseled body was throbbing against me as his hands ran up and down my body. Massaging my breast and gripping my hips. Hiking my thighs up his legs until there was nothing supporting me but his chest against my body. His hands grasped my ass, and my hands flew around his neck. Our teeth clattered together, and I was ready for him to take me.

In any way he wished.

He peeled me away from the glass and carried me into his bedroom. Our hands began to strip one another down, tossing shirts and bras and ties off to the side. I ran my hands along the strength of him. I could feel his lips in places I'd wanted him for days. Weeks.

And if I was honest with myself, months.

His five o'clock shadow grazed down my chest as he laid me on the bed. I could feel my arousal dripping down my ass as his hands parted my legs. I bucked into him and arched, trying to feel more of him as his lips wrapped around my nipples. His lips sucked them to painful peaks, and his teeth bit down lightly onto them, throwing me into a tailspin of endless moans and whispered praises.

I rolled him over, taking him by surprise. I grinned down at his shocked face as he reached up to remove my glasses. He tossed them off the bed, clunking to the ground as his thick dick pulsed between my legs.

Then, I rolled my hips and captured him within the folds of my pussy.

Inch by inch, he sank into me. His hands gripped my hips, embedding his fingerprints into my skin. My hands curled into his chest, taking in the divots of his muscles as he filled me to capacity.

He pressed against my tight walls in ways I'd never felt before.

Before I could set a steady pace, he flipped me back over. I was on my back, squealing with delight as he hiked my legs around his body. He slid from within me, leaving nothing but the tip of his cock seated between my legs.

Then he slammed into my body, pulling goosebumps along every limb I had.

He sent a relentless pace as his name tumbled from my lips. The fire in my gut was burning up every atom of my skin. He felt so good, so big inside of my body. He hit areas I didn't know existed, and his tightly wound curls raked against my clit. My legs jolted with every movement as my lips fell against his chest. I bit at his skin and raked at his arms, desperate to feel any part of him in any way he would let me.

He picked me up off the bed and pinned me to the wall. His hips snapped against mine as I clung to his body. I buried my face into his neck, gasping for air and begging for more. I adored the feeling of him within me and the electricity that coursed through my veins as my blood rushed through my ears.

He pulled me from the wall and tossed my body onto the bed. I caught myself with my hands but not before my hips were thrust into the air. He plunged into me from behind, not allowing me to stop and take any breath before he fucked me senseless. His hips snapped against mine so hard, his balls were slapping against my skin.

"Jimmy. Jimmy. Holy... I... don't stop. I've wait—oh... Right there. Right there. Right there, Jimmy. Please!"

I could hear him grunting as he bent over my body, hovering above me like an animal in heat. I looked up into the window and saw his reflection, the way his face was twisted with pleasure. His lips fell to my skin as he pounded against me, building that fire behind my abs that threatened to burst forth. His lips kissed each divot of my spine as his hands held me to him, fucking me senseless as my pussy throbbed around his cock.

"I feel you, Ashley. All of you. Let go. Give into me. I know you can."

His encouragement sent me spiraling as my toes began to curl. I fisted the sheets of his bed and moaned out into the room, my pussy clamping down on him. I felt his movements stuttering against me as my jaw unhinged. I choked out my moans and wrapped my feet around his legs, pulling him to me as he collapsed.

His sweating chest hit my back and the two of us plummeted to the bed, his cock sliding from me and pumping his come onto the sheets of his bed.

His hands slid down my arms, lacing our fingers together at the end. I relished the feeling of him blanketing me, coating me in his warmth as my head undulated with relaxation. I hadn't felt this good in a long time, not since the night we had shared together. There were things that compared. Like my promotion or finding out he'd ended things with Nina.

But nothing quite compared to this.

Nothing compared to the feeling of electric pleasure coursing through my skin.

Jimmy kissed my shoulder before he slid from me and pulled me into his embrace. He wiggled us out of the wet spot and held me close to him, my leg tossed over his body. I laid my cheek against his chest and listened to his heartbeat, rapid and strong, racing with the exertion it had taken to please me.

I kissed his racing heart and watched as his skin puckered again with arousal.

"You could stay, if you wanted," Jimmy said.

"I know," I said. "But I can't."

"Still worried about Nina?" he asked.

"Actually, no. But I have to take my mother to a doctor's appointment in the morning. Well, I want to. I don't have to take her, but I want to take her."

"I understand," he said. "I'd never keep you from something like that, but just so you know, I'd take you wherever you needed to go."

"Thanks, Jimmy. I really do appreciate it."

I felt his hand running through the tendrils of my hair. His touch was soft, which was a stark contrast to the animal I'd experienced only moments before. I sighed against his skin, relishing the moment before I had to break it.

"You never told me why your mom fell that day," Jimmy said.

"I told you. She took a fall," I said.

"What caused the fall?"

I sighed as I closed my eyes, my brain paying attention to Jimmy's hand and how rhythmically he stroked my hair, how strong his heartbeat was, how comforting his body felt against mine, and how steadfast his strength felt.

He was breaking down my walls, and I didn't know how to stop it.

"My mother has Alzheimer's," I said.

"I'm so sorry," Jimmy said.

"She's had it for a few years now, about six."

I felt his grasp tighten around me, and I snuggled tighter into the side of his body. I wanted his comfort, and I'd never experienced that before. I was used to standing on my own and receiving pity from no one.

But I enjoyed him comforting me. His hand stroked up and down my back, and his lips connected with my forehead.

It was like he wanted to hear about this part of my life.

"I took care of her in my childhood apartment for a while, but it became too much," I said. "Her memory got worse, and her lucid moments got shorter. I couldn't hold down the job I had at your company and still take care of her."

"So you put her in a home," Jimmy said.

"Not just any home. The best nursing home in Miami, but even with her being on Medicaid, it's got a hefty premium each month. I saved everything I could from my job to pay for it."

I felt him pull me closer as my buried my face into his neck.

"You're a good daughter, Ashley," he said.

"I don't feel like it some days. It's why I want to take her to these doctor's appointments. Her lucid moments are so few and far between, I don't want to risk not being there for one of them. I don't want to risk her being lucid and not seeing me there, thinking I abandoned her or something."

"You have nothing to explain to me," he said. "But thank you for talking about it. You know you can put her on your insurance, right?"

"What?" I asked.

"If you can prove you pay at least fifty percent of her bills—and it sounds like you pay almost all of them—she can go on your insurance through the company."

"She can?" I asked.

"Yep. She'll still keep her Medicaid, and the company's policy should cover any holes in her plan."

"Are you serious, Jimmy?"

I looked into his eyes before I thrust my lips to his. I had landed in this promotion so quickly, I hadn't stopped to consider how my benefits had changed, how my health insurance had changed, and how my retirement fund was going to benefit from all this. His hand tangled in my hair, and my body rolled on top of his. I felt tears crest my eyes as he pulled my lips away, our eyes connecting as tears dripping down my cheeks.

"You have those benefits through the company, but you also have me. If there's anything I can do to make your mother comfortable and to make any of this easier for you, all you have to do is ask," Jimmy said.

"You have no idea what you've just done," I said breathlessly. "Thank you."

"Don't thank me. It's a perk that comes with the health benefits of corporate. My hope one day is to make that kind of health insurance available to the rest of the company."

"You're a good man," I said.

"And you're a good woman, Ashley. And a good daughter. And a hell of an accountant."

Our foreheads connected as a small smile crossed my cheeks.

"I should get going if I'm going to get rest for tomorrow," I said.

"Sure there's nothing I can do to convince you to stay?"

"We'll work our way toward it," I said.

"That's all I can ever ask of you."

I slid from his body and began putting my clothes on. Jimmy was already on the phone with someone, talking them through the change in my health insurance. I shook my head as I pulled my shirt back on, my eyes raking up and down his naked form.

He really was a beautiful man.

"Once you get back from taking your mother to the doctor, some papers will be on your desk for you to sign. Look them over, sign them, and get them to HR. They'll push the necessary changes through, and your mother should be covered through us by the end of the week."

"Thank you," I said. "From the bottom of my heart."

"Let's just say you owe me a dinner."

He winked at me, and I felt my cheeks blush. He pulled on his pants and walked me to his door. He gave me one last kiss good night before I pulled out my phone, ready to summon a car from Uber.

But his hand came down on mine, and he covered the screen of my cell phone.

"Did you think I wouldn't get you home?" Jimmy asked.

"You mean you're going to drive me home like this?" I asked.

"Not necessarily. If I drive you home, you might not get to sleep after all. I know my limits, and you test them every day. But my driver's waiting for you downstairs out front. He'll be ready to take you anywhere you want to go."

"That's really not necessary. I can just call—"

"I love that you fight me on these things, but let this be one you give me without a fight. I want to make sure you get home safely. Your car's still at work, and he'll see to it you get there and get in without being disturbed."

I smiled up at Jimmy, blushing as his thumb stroked my cheek.

"You better go before I don't let you," he said.

"I don't think you have that kind of power over me."

His eyes darkened as his hand wrapped around to the back of my neck. He tightened his grip, and I sighed, my body instantly caving to him. I cursed myself as my eyes fluttered open, and I found that shit-eating grin on his cheeks.

"Good night, Miss Ternbeau."

And I walked with weakened knees all the way to the elevator.

Chapter 5

Jimmy

"To new ventures," Ross said.

"To new ventures," I said.

I clinked my glass bottle with Ross before the two of us settled back. Ashley had taken off the rest of the day at work to be with her mother after her doctor's appointment. I wasn't sure what had spawned the change in her decision, but it didn't matter. She sounded okay, and she said she didn't need anything, so I needed to take her word at that. I was more than happy to give her the time off to spend with her mother, especially if her mother was having a good day.

I couldn't imagine watching someone I loved waste away like that.

"Thanks for inviting me out," I said.

"I don't usually see you drinking beers," Ross said. "Good day?"

"Very good day. Guess who's coming into town?" I asked.

"Let me guess. Markus."

"Hell, yeah, Markus. He flies in tomorrow, and we're supposed to be getting drinks."

"It's about time he came in. He's been gone for a while."

"A little over a year, despite the money he still invests."

"He planning on making a stop by the company?" he asked.

"I'm sure he will. He's flying in on business of his own, so I don't know what his exact schedule is, but Markus has never been the kind of man to drop in unannounced."

"Oh, no. Markus enjoys the pomp and circumstance."

"Can't fault the man for that, especially after his divorce."

"Yes. Learn from that man's mistakes," Ross said.

"Hence why Nina is gone."

"I'd like to think I had something to do with that, but I'll take it," he said.

"To Markus coming into town and regaling us with whatever insane stories he has for us this time," I said.

But before Ross could cheer Markus's temporary homecoming, the news station on the television caught my attention.

"Is that you?" Ross asked.

"What the fuck is my picture doing on the news?" I asked.

"Bartender. Can you turn that up?" he asked.

I felt my stomach hit my toes as my Twitter feed popped up on the news.

"Sources say Jimmy Sheldon, founder and CEO of Big Steps, has been bribing followers on his social media pages. The accusations state that Mr. Sheldon has been shelling out his own money to get people to favor and buy his product. I'm sure his competitors won't be happy when they find out Mr. Sheldon is being accused of undercutting the competition."

"What the fuck is that?" I asked. "Ross, did you know something about this?"

"This has Nina written all over it," Ross said.

"That little—"

"Watch it. People are staring," he said.

I looked around the bar and found everyone's eyes geared toward me. We had to get out of there. I had to instate damage control. I threw back the rest of my beer while Ross threw some money onto our table, and then the two of us started for our car. We hopped in just as my cell phone rang, and I didn't have to look at the screen to know who was calling.

"Have you seen the news?" Ashley said.

"Just saw it. In a bar full of people," I said.

"You know who this is, right?" she asked.

"It's Nina," Ross said.

"Ross is with you? Good. The two of you need to get back to the office and start coordinating a plan of attack," Ashley said.

"You sound like my public relations correspondent," I said.

"Have you called her? Sherry, right?" she asked.

"Yep. Ross is calling Sherry right now," I said.

I shot Ross a look, and he dug out his phone, placing the phone call to say she should get into the office immediately.

"Does this claim have any merit?" Ashley asked.

"Of course not," I said. "Nina's only trying to hurt me. She's mad, and instead of taking the loss and making her own way in life, she's choosing the revenge route."

"Do I need to be worried?" she asked.

"No. The last person she'll touch is you. I won't allow it. That woman will go down in history if she tries to mess with you."

"If she's trying to hurt you, she could come after me."

"I don't care what she does, but you need to understand she won't do that. She knows me better than that. She knows you're off-limits. I'll bring everything down on her head in a heartbeat if she comes at you," I said. "What I did in the restaurant that night was kind. Calm. Like flicking an ant off a sofa cushion."

"Jimmy, I know you're upset, but try to think about this logically. If she's trying to ruin your image, she might not have any issues exposing the arrangement you had with her."

Ashley had a point, and it was a point I couldn't ignore.

"Nina has to accept that we're over. Part of me thinks maybe she's acting this way because she did develop feelings, but the feelings weren't reciprocated. No matter where this is coming from, Nina has to accept that our arrangement-slash-relationship is over," I said.

"I told you we needed to be worried about her," she said.

"And now we have reason to worry. I'll be on my guard, but you shouldn't be. I want to be with you, and that means protecting you if necessary. You will be okay. Do you hear me?"

"I do. I hear you. Just think about coming clean."

"What?" I asked.

"About your arrangement with Nina. Think about coming clean, telling the public the truth. It's going to be easier to come back from that than it will be if she reveals it."

"Telling the public the truth would be annihilation, Ashley."

"But then you could tell them about how you wanted to be with me. It's the story of a cold-hearted businessman who morphed into a man who wanted to find something real. The crowd likes those kinds of stories, and it isn't far from the truth."

"Should I hire you as my PR representative as well?" I asked.

"Hardly. But it's simple fact. She can't use anything against you that you expose yourself. Own up to what the relationship was, and be honest about why you decided to end it. You take her biggest weapon away, and she looks like the spiteful gold digger."

"I have to say, I'm enjoying this side of you. How's your mother?" I asked.

"She had a really good day today. Thank you for giving me the day off with her."

"I told you, you already had it. You were the one choosing to come to work."

"Whatever. Anyway, get off here and go fix your world. Think about what I said. I'll support you in whatever decision you make, but Nina isn't to be messed with. She's making good on that threat of making you pay. This is serious."

"I know. I hear you. I gotta go. Ross is trying to tell me something," I said.

"See you in the morning, Jimmy."

"See you then, Ashley."

"I got Sherry on the line. She's arranging a press conference for tomorrow," Ross said.

"Good. Okay. Tell her to prepare the press conference for first thing in the morning. I'm releasing all my social media streams and private messages for the public and potential clients to scour. We're going to investigate this claim and figure out who made it, though we pretty much know who did. Once we can prove it, though, we're suing."

"Do you want to tell the public that?"

"Yes," I said. "Tell Sherry."

"So, we aren't running with Ashley's plan?" he asked.

"While it's a good plan, it's suicide, and if this isn't Nina for some weird reason, the last thing I want is to start a war with that woman. We figure out the truth, and then we sue like any other company would do. Ashley's plan, while creative, is too shortsighted, and we don't have enough information to throw ourselves into that fire safely yet."

"Okay. I'll let Sherry know," Ross said.

Chapter 6

Ashley

I watched from the sidelines as the press conference was about to begin. I kept chewing on my nails as I scanned the crowd for Nina. There were so many people here waiting for Jimmy's statement. The outrage had grown overnight to a point where people were picketing outside of his headquarters. In this current social climate, things like this were taken very seriously. Part of me was hoping he wouldn't use my tactic. What he needed was to put up a strong front, to take charge of this situation and try to calm the public about his business dealings, not going around revealing his personal life and opening himself up to danger.

Part of me had suggested that for selfish reasons. Jimmy and I were dating officially but not openly. His and Nina's breakup still hadn't been reported to the news, so for all intents and purposes, the two of them were still together. The moment I hung up the phone with him last night, I felt sick to my stomach with guilt at how I was right and how I had allowed my jealousy to somehow creep into the picture.

This wasn't about me. It was about Jimmy and his company.

"For those of you who are here, I thank you for coming. Big Steps has seen a lot of success over the past few years, so it only stands to reason that someone would want to strike at the core of that. I know a lot of people are outraged by the accusations made against me last night, and if this was someone else's company I would be just as outraged. So here's what I'm doing. Right now, my tech department is releasing all my social media direct messages. Instagram, Twitter, and my Facebook business page. They're going to be posted all online in a database for any concerned customer or potential customer to read through. Never once have I bribed anyone to purchase my product. Big Steps and I take pride in having our product speak for itself. The database of direct messages should be up for the public to view within the next couple of minutes, and then my lawyers will get to work on investigating the false claims made against my company. We're taking this accusation seriously, and whoever is responsible for this claim will be sued accordingly. No one can walk around filing false reports with the police, and no one can walk around making false assumptions about someone's business practices. I hope to be fully transparent to the public and swift in my legal action against the person who decided to try to negate all the hard work Big Steps and its employees have indulged in over the years. By the end of the day, I promise you these accusations will be cleared up and the proper papers served to the proper individual. In the meantime, feel free to browse the database."

Jimmy stepped off the podium without answering any questions. He buttoned his suit coat and turned to me, his eyes beckoning me to follow him. Ross fell in line beside him, and I walked up to the other side, following him back into the building.

The moment we got into his office, I shut his door and threw my arms around his neck.

"I'm so sorry," I said.

"For what?" Jimmy asked

He slid his arms around me, holding me tighter than he ever had before.

"For giving you that crappy advice. For all this stuff you're going through. For Nina and all of ... everything."

"First off, your advice wasn't crappy. It was a good tactic. Just one we didn't have enough information to safely take. While we all assume it's Nina, there are many people jealous of my success, businessmen who have never been able to keep up who would love to take a strike at me. If I'm going to use a weapon like you suggested, I have to have proof. I have to be sure it's Nina before starting that war with her."

"Part of it was out of selfishness on my part," I said. "I want Nina to be put behind us so we can ... you know."

I dipped my head down before his finger caught my chin.

"Look at me, Ashley."

I lifted my gaze to his and got lost in his eyes.

"I know," he said. "I've put you in a terrible situation, but I'm navigating it as fast as I can. I know you're tired of sneaking around and having to avoid restaurants that allow photographers to take pictures of people. I know some of your favorite restaurants are those types of restaurants. I promise you, the time will come."

"I'm sorry," I said.

"Stop apologizing. You have nothing to be sorry for," he said.

There was a knock on Jimmy's door, and I took a step away from him. He cleared his throat and situated his tie, smoothing his hands down his suit. I grinned at him as I turned toward the door, taking deep breaths to try and calm the blush on my cheeks.

"Come in," Jimmy said.

"Hell of a press conference," the man said. "Sucks to be going through, though."

"Markus. You were supposed to call me when you landed."

A man in his fifties embraced Jimmy tightly. He was an attractive man, alluring if that was a woman's thing. White hair at his temples faded into his jet-black hair, and his deep brown eyes commanded a room with one look around it. He was Jimmy's height, but his body was broader and stronger, not toned like Jimmy's but stacked with muscle.

I didn't recognize him, but I recognized his name.

"So this is Markus," I said.

"And you must be Ashley," he said. "It's a pleasure to meet you."

I shook the man's hand, and he gave me a kind smile. It was odd. He was this mixture of tough and firm but gentle in his eyes. Commanding, but relaxing. I felt confused looking at him, tense but excited at the same time.

And the look on Jimmy's face. He was beaming like a son who was proud of his father. I'd never seem Jimmy smile in the presence of someone like that before.

This man was obviously very important to him.

"Will you be staying with us this morning?" Markus asked.

"Oh, no. An accountant's work is never done. I've got balance sheets galore and investors expecting updates," I said.

"Am I supposed to be getting that PDF today? I swear, it's much more convenient than those damn packets you used to send out, Jimmy."

"I better go get started on them," I said. "It was really nice meeting you."

"And you as well. I hope we run into one another soon. I want to get to know the woman who finally made Jimmy dump that witch."

"Ah, another Nina fan, I see."

The three of us shared a laugh before I slipped out the door.

I did have a lot of work ahead of me. With the scandal that broke on Jimmy last night, it had me worried about the irregularities I was finding on the balance sheets. I still didn't have a reason for them, but there were many of them, multiple ones on multiple pages, and they only kept multiplying. Even the most basic of accountant would've been able to catch these downstairs, so it made me think it wasn't user error.

But my fear was that it also wasn't a technological error, either.

The irregularities weren't only current, though. The greater they became, the more I began to dig back into the company's history. That was the benefit of being the head honcho accountant in corporate. I could access almost anything with my badge, username, and password. I was pulling up balance sheets and printing them off. I was spending late nights in the office running figures in my head. I was taking this stuff home and curling up with Chipper and continuing to count out numbers in my head.

And the irregularities didn't stop.

They dated all the way back to the inception of the company.

The irregularities themselves were small. There weren't thousands of dollars missing at any one given moment. Totals were being fudged to cover thirty and forty dollars going missing, or fifty dollars being slipped into an account and not being noted on the balance sheets. It was easy to miss those small numbers, especially in the beginning of a company. These balance sheets were done once a quarter, so it wasn't like other people had the luxury of looking at them all at once like I could.

But it was still odd to me that everyone missed this from the start of the company.

I kept flipping through documents whenever I wasn't working on stuff for the investors. I sent out the PDFs with projected earnings despite the scandal and sent reassurances that things were okay and stable. I worked through lunch again and occasionally heard Markus and Jimmy laughing in his office, and it would give me pause. The happiness that fell from Jimmy's voice made me smile. I was looking forward to getting to know Markus, whenever that chance might be.

Six o'clock rolled around, and my back was beginning to ache. I needed to go get Chipper from the doggie resort I signed him up for, and I wanted to stop in on my mom one last time. I printed out the final balance sheet—the very first one the company ever had—and sighed when I found more irregularities.

The totals never breached fifty dollars per transaction, but there were a lot of them.

I needed to tell Jimmy. I needed to take all of this to him and go through it with him. But with Markus in town and him getting a bit of relief from all this stress, I figured it could wait. I didn't want to ruin his happiness with yet more issues with his company, and there was still some research I could do to rule some things out.

I slipped the file folders of balance sheets into my desk and locked it and then gathered up my things. Monday would be a good day to bring it up to Jimmy. He would get some time with Markus, things with this social media issue would settle down, and we could tackle it head-on together.

Monday.

Not tonight.

Chapter 7

Jimmy

I picked Ashley up for our wonderful dinner ahead. I couldn't wait for her to get to know Markus. I hadn't given a damn about introducing Nina to him, but I really wanted Ashley to get to know him and to like him the way I did. I felt nervous like a guy introducing his girlfriend to his dad.

But the moment Ashley opened the door, she robbed the breath from my lungs.

She was in this gorgeous dress. The navy-blue bodice framed her breasts perfectly before cinching in just underneath them. The skirt fell all the way to her feet, stripped with whites and yellows and deep reds. The colors made her hair and eyes pop, and she looked absolutely radiant in the light of the moon.

"Ready for dinner?" she asked.

"You look spectacular," I said.

I offered her my arm, and we made our way to dinner. I drove us across town and led us to the table that Ross and Markus were already sitting at. There was a very young woman at his side. Pretty little thing. Long black hair that matched his and dark hazel eyes. The kind that changed colors with whatever she was wearing. But her age wasn't something I was going to judge. She was leaning into Markus, and he was whispering in her ear. I hadn't seen him with a woman since his divorce from his arranged wife, and it was nice to see him cradling a girl who seemed to make him happy.

So I was happy for him.

"Jimmy Sheldon," I said as I introduced myself. "This is Ross Fowler, and this lovely lady is Ashley Ternbeau."

"It's nice to meet you," Ashley said.

"Jamie Scott. I'm sorry if I'm intruding. Markus told me it was okay to come, but I still wasn't sure," she said.

"The more the merrier," Ross said with a smile.

"You're welcome among us anytime," I said.

"So, Miss Ashley, I hear you've caught the eye of Jimmy here," Markus said.

"I'm not sure if 'caught' is the right word. Possibly stolen after a few too many drinks," Ashley said.

"That sounds more like the Jimmy I know. He can't keep his hands off a beautiful woman once he gets going," Markus said.

"Sounds like there's a story to be told," Ashley said.

"If it's the one I'm thinking about, we can definitely leave that to another day," I said.

"See? Now I have to know," Ashley said.

"Oh, I like her," Markus said. "One time at the beginning of his company, I convinced him to throw a party to celebrate their first large customer and give his employees a real blowout bash."

"You're the mind behind the parties," Ashley said.

I squeezed her knee and felt her skin pucker underneath her dress.

"Nice to know traditions are still carried on. But, at this party, he kept throwing back shots of tequila."

"Tequila? I've never seen him drink tequila," Ashley said.

"Not after that party, nope," Markus said. "He got drunk enough to hit on one of his first investors. A beautiful woman. A bit old for him, but still a looker. He tried dancing with her and went to dip her, and she knocked her head against the tiled floor. She went to the hospital with a concussion."

"No, she didn't," Ashley said. "You did not."

"That was a hell of a party," Ross said.

Ashley threw her head back and laughed. I enjoyed watching her interact with Markus and enjoy him like I had over the years. I'd missed him. I wished he came into town more often. He was my very first investor in my company and the man who guided me throughout all the biggest decisions I'd made as a businessman. He was the father I never had, the father I wished I'd had when I was growing up. I hated that he had moved to Canada to set up his headquarters, but I understood. Canada fit his needs more than Miami or even the East Coast did.

But that didn't mean I couldn't miss him.

"How long have you been working for the company, Ashley?" Markus asked.

"About four years, but I recently took a new position as—"

"Account Rep for the investors," Markus said.

"I see someone's been talking about me," Ashley said.

"You're his favorite topic when he's not talking about work," Ross said.

"Or avoiding tequila," Jamie said.

The five of us laughed at her joke before she stuck her foot in her mouth.

"Though I have to ask. What happened with Nina? The two of you looked so happy together."

Ashley looked over at me as my eyes connected with the woman at Markus's side. Ashley placed her hand on top of mine on her knee and squeezed, trying to get me to calm down. I felt the wave of anger rearing its head throughout my body, but this wasn't the time to cause a scene. It was a question I knew would come up eventually, and I needed to go ahead and smooth things over. Get the conversation started.

At least she hadn't asked about my wedding ring.

"Relationships come and go, but the ones that are important are the ones I tend to cling to. My relationship with Ashley is more than simply romantic, and I'm lucky she's at my side."

"Oh, that's so sweet," Jamie said with a smile. "Markus, isn't that sweet?"

"Not as sweet as you, beautiful," Markus said. "Nothing's as sweet as you."

The two of them shared a kiss, and I looked down at Ashley. I watched her eyes light up as she took in their moment, and I chanced a kiss on top of her head. She looked up at me with those sparkling eyes behind those thick-rimmed glasses of hers.

This evening couldn't get any better.

After three hours of drinking and eating and catching up, it was time for us to part ways. Jamie was yawning on Markus's shoulder, and Ashley seemed to be fading a bit as well. Everyone said their goodbyes before I led Ashley to my car and drove us back to my place.

I enjoyed the way she had looked in it the first time I'd brought her home.

"Would you care for a glass of wine?" I asked.

"I think one more might be okay," she said.

"Red or white?" I asked.

"Whichever you're having is fine."

"So, what did you think of Markus?" I asked.

Ashley reached out for her glass as I settled beside her on the couch.

"He seems really nice, and I can tell he's fond of you."

"I'm fond of him. He's an important person to me," I said.

"I think he's charming, and you can tell there's something there between him and Jamie. Is it odd that their age difference shocked me, though?"

"Not odd," I said. "I was taken aback as well. But they both seem happy, and that's all that matters."

"I hope they make it. They seem really sweet together," she said.

"Do you think you'd like to go out with Markus and me again while he's in town?"

"Of course, I would. In a way, I feel like I'm getting to know your father. Though I know he's not actually your father," she said.

"He's like a father. He's been with me for a long time in this company. First investor, advice-giver, the whole nine. He's a good man, and I'm glad you like him. I was nervous you wouldn't."

"Why wouldn't I? He's charming and sweet. Obviously, knows how to make people feel comfortable around him. What's not to like?"

"You've never witnessed him in a boardroom meeting with his company," I said with a grin.

"And hopefully, I never will because I don't like that grin on your face."

Ashley settled into my arms as we each finished our glasses of wine. I saw her eyes drooping as she cradled into me, her legs coming up to rest on the couch. Part of me didn't want to move us because of her falling asleep. I was excited at the prospect of her staying over, but neither of us was going to get a good night's sleep if we tried to do it on the couch.

So I shifted her head and picked her up in my arms.

"Where we going?" Ashley asked.

"Figured sleeping in the bed might be a bit more comfortable," I said.

"Mmm, okay."

I grinned as I laid her down in bed and then watched her lazily kick her heels off. I plucked her glasses from her face and set them down on the nightstand. She looked so peaceful curled up underneath the blankets of my bed.

The sight was heavenly.

I undressed and tossed my suit over a chair in the corner. I slipped in beside her in nothing but my boxers, hoping I wasn't crossing a line with her. This was a first for us, spending the night with one another. My arm wrapped around her, and I pulled her close to me, feeling her ass wiggle against my pelvis.

"You might wanna be careful with that," I said into her ear. "That's a weapon you're flinging around."

She turned in my arms as a sleepy smile crossed her face. Her hand came up to my cheek, and she brought my lips to hers. I could taste the wine on her tongue. The spice of the alcohol against her cheek. I slid on top of her as her hands tangled in my hair, her legs opening up to me.

I kissed every exposed part of her. My lips trailed along her cheeks and her neck. I nuzzled my nose against her exposed breasts as her lips kissed my forehead. I sank myself into her, breathing in her scent as her hands ran through my hair.

"I never thanked you for the other night," Ashley said.

"Which one?" I asked.

"The one at my apartment. With that fun little gift you gave me."

"No thanks needed. Though I meant what I said about working up your tolerance."

Ashley giggled a sleepy little giggle as I looked up at her. She looked peaceful. Content. With a happy little smile on her cheeks. Her eyes were closed, and her chest was steadily rising and falling. Her grip was already growing lax against me as I shifted on top of her body. I fell back to the side and pulled her close, tucking her head underneath my chin.

I wanted things to stay like this between us, as innocent and as new as our first time together.

Chapter 8

Ashley

My eyes fluttered open as the sun poured through the window. I felt Jimmy's warm body underneath mine, and a smile crossed my cheeks. It felt so good being in his arms, cradled against his strong body all night. It was so nice that we could finally be together like this after navigating the first question of Nina and officially putting it out there that they were no longer together.

I nuzzled into him, and his grip tightened on me. He groaned and rolled over, his nose connecting with mine. He was so handsome, especially with his hair mussed with sleep. I ran my hand through it, watching as his nose scrunched up.

I did it a few more times, taking in the involuntary movement before his eyes slid open.

"Good morning," I said.

"What a wonderful sight."

His voice was heavy with sleep, and it shot chills down my spine.

"Sleep well?" I asked.

"Better than I have in a long time," Jimmy said. "You?"

"With ease," I said. "I figured I could get up and make us some coffee."

But before I could move, Jimmy threw his arms around me.

"You're not getting out of this bed," he said.

"But I need caffeine."

"And I need you," he said. "Right here. Next to me."

I froze at his words and allowed them to descend on my mind. Did he mean what he had just said? I scooted on top of his body and pressed a kiss to his neck. His groan caused me to plant another one, and another, and yet another still. I kept kissing him until his hands were running up and down my back and his cock was pressing into my thigh.

Then our lips connected, and I could feel the truth behind them.

"If you're not careful, you might get something you didn't bargain for," Jimmy said.

"Coffee first. Then we can talk," I said with a grin.

With a fake sigh and an exaggerated eye roll, Jimmy got out of bed. I followed him into the kitchen and sat at his breakfast nook, watching as he started to make coffee. His long legs were flexing with strength, and his languid arms were long and dexterous. Every movement he made was done with a grace I'd never seen in a man before. The strength of his back was pulling against his bare skin, and every time he turned to me, my eyes fell to his abs.

Jimmy was a beautiful man.

And he was all mine.

"Like what you see?" he asked.

"You're full of it," I said.

"Don't worry. I like what I see too," he said.

I looked down and saw that I was a shake away from spilling out of my top. I gasped with shock and tucked myself back into my dress as a chuckle fell from Jimmy's lips. My face flushed with embarrassment as the coffee began to percolate, and I felt his hands cup my cheeks and raise my gaze to his.

"You're a beautiful woman, Ashley. Never hide that from me."

"I was almost out of my dress," I said.

"And it isn't anything I would've complained about," he said with a wink.

I shook my head as the coffee finished up, and he made a mug especially for me. The tired silence between the two of us was comfortable, and a fleeting thought crossed my mind.

I could get used to this.

I sniffed in the glorious smell and gazed at the man in front of me. His legs were tangled with mine underneath the table as we stared into one another's eyes. It was amazing, how I could feel so vulnerable and exposed yet so comfortable in that state around him. He grinned at me from beyond his mug, and I blushed. Then, a familiar sound caught my ear.

"I think my phone's ringing," I said.

"Hold on. I'll get it for you."

Jimmy got up from the nook, and I watched him walk away from me. His ass was nice and tight, filling out his boxers as his shoulders flexed. How that man could be as gorgeous as he was confused me to my core. A man like him shouldn't exist.

It should've been illegal.

I took my phone from Jimmy, and he sat back down across from me. I furrowed my brow at the number and then picked up my phone.

And the peaceful morning I was sharing was shot.

"Hello?" I asked.

"Hey there, Ashley."

"Mom?"

"Yes, it's Mom. Who else would it be from this number? I need help getting some groceries for our meals this week, and I was wondering if you could come over and help."

I felt my heart sink as I held out my phone and took another look at the number.

She was calling from her room in the nursing home.

"Mom, are you sure you need to go get groceries?" I asked.

I watched Jimmy's eyes go from playful to worried in a split second.

"Of course, we need groceries, Ashley. How am I going to cook meatloaf without any breadcrumbs?" my mother asked.

"Okay, Mom. I didn't realize we didn't have breadcrumbs. I'll come pick you up, okay?"

"That's fine, but hurry on over. I want to beat the Monday morning slouchers."

I wanted to tell my mother it was Saturday, but I decided against it.

I hung up the phone and threw back the rest of my coffee. Standing up from the nook, I strode to Jimmy's room to slip into my heels and walked into his bathroom, running my fingers through my hair. I reached for a cotton swab and ran it under some water to touch up the makeup I'd gotten smeared everywhere, and all the while, Jimmy was watching me from the doorway of his bathroom.

"I need to go see my mother," I said.

"I wasn't going to stop you from that. You know this," he said.

"She must not be having a good day," I said.

"Just let me know where to take you, and we'll be there."

"Jimmy, this isn't—"

"I'm not asking to meet her. I'm simply asking you to let me tag along for moral support for you. I can't imagine what you're going through, and I want to be there for you during those times. Allow me that."

I looked over at him, and his stern eyes buckled my resolve. I nodded, and he pushed off the doorway, heading for the suit he wore last night. He was dressed faster than I could get myself together, and I helped myself to his mouthwash to try and make my breath a little more presentable.

"Sorry," I said as I spit.

"Don't be. Help yourself to anything. I'm ready when you are," Jimmy said.

"You don't wanna brush your teeth or anything?" I asked.

"I'll keep a safe distance. Your mother's more important right now."

My heart melted as he held his arm out for me. The two of us made our way to his car, and I showed him where to go. We pulled into the parking lot, and I told him to stay there. Then, I got out and went into the nursing home.

Everyone was gathered at the front door trying to calm my mother down.

"You don't understand. My daughter's picking me up. We're going grocery shopping."

"Hey there, Mom."

The nurses all shot me a sympathetic look as I reached out and took her hands.

"What took you so long? The Monday slouchers are going to be there, and we're going to get caught up in their slow lines," my mother said.

"Mom, it's Saturday," I said.

"Oh. Well, then we're in the middle of the Saturday morning rush. Your father doesn't understand these things. Thinks I'm crazy and overbearing, but it's true. Certain types of people shop on certain days, and you never want to get caught up in it."

"Mom, you don't have to go grocery shopping," I said.

"And why not?" she asked.

"Because you're in a nursing home, remember? We sold the apartment two years ago?"

I watched a blank stare come across my mother's face before she started looking around her, taking in the white walls with colorful decorations and the nurses standing around us. I could tell she couldn't remember. I could tell she was struggling. The smile on her face was empty as she turned her gaze back to me, her hands sliding from mine.

"Oh, yeah, I know that," my mother said. "Why wouldn't you think I know that?"

"How about we go back to your room, and I'll tell you all about my week, okay?" I asked. "Maybe have someone bring us a snack?"

"A snack might be nice. Maybe some pudding or some crackers."

"That sounds really good. Why don't you follow this nice lady here, and I'll be there in a second," I said.

I watched the two of them walk away before I turned my head to the woman standing next to me.

"How do you think she would handle company?" I asked.

"What do you mean?" the nurse asked.

"I have someone here who wants to meet her, a guy I've been seeing."

"Good for you," the nurse said.

"But I'm not sure if she's up for it," I said.

"I think she'll be okay. She's been partially lucid like this for most of the day, but we couldn't get her to back down from the groceries. Seeing someone new might do her some good."

"Okay," I said. "That ... that sounds good."

I went out to the car and beckoned for Jimmy. He got out in his tailored suit, and I could see people already beginning to stare. I pushed him into the nursing room, and the women at the front desk were drooling over him.

I felt a small surge of pride fill my chest as we walked down the hallway.

"Mom?" I asked. "Can I come in?"

"Ashley?" she asked. "When did you get here?"

I threw a look up to Jimmy, and he tucked my hair behind my ear. His touch was so comforting during something like this, and his hand fell to the small of my back. He didn't push me into the room or try to lead me in any way. He was waiting for my permission, waiting for my lead.

"There's someone I want you to meet," I said.

My mother turned her head as Jimmy and I entered the room.

"Well, it's about time you introduced me to this husband of yours. And he's handsome too."

"Oh, Mom. No. This is—"

"Jimmy Sheldon. It's wonderful to meet you," he said.

"And polite. I never thought my daughter would find someone. How did you get her out of the apartment?" she asked.

"A little bit of dinner and the promise of wine," Jimmy said.

"You better not be pumping my daughter full of alcohol for your own selfish purposes. I may look fragile, but I know a thing or two about the delicate form of the male body."

I felt my eyes widen as Jimmy sat down next to her.

"I don't know why Ashley insisted on not introducing us sooner. I hardly got to know you before the wedding."

"No. Mom. You don't—"

But Jimmy held up his hand before a smile crossed his cheeks.

"That's my fault. I travel a lot for my work. I'm a businessman, and it takes me all over the world."

"But not into the arms of other women, I hope. You'd have to answer to me if that happened," my mother said.

"Never. Your daughter never has to worry about that with me."

"The wedding was so beautiful, Jimmy. Those flowers hanging from the ceiling and that white tuxedo you were in. Oh, it made me so happy."

"Did you like Ashley's wedding dress? I thought the princess look was perfect for her," he said.

I sat on the empty bed beside my mother's and watched Jimmy curl his hand around my mother's. She was hallucinating everything, drawing off a mixture of dreams and memories from her own past, and Jimmy was rolling with it like nothing was wrong.

"The train was a bit long, but it was beautiful. And the reception. Oh! The food. I've never tasted food like that in my life."

"Had it flown in from Cuba," Jimmy said. "Did you like the spice to the fish?"

"Yes, I did. Ate way too much of it, if you ask me. I had no room for cake afterward."

"I hope you took a slice with you. It was decadent," he said.

He looked up at me, and I tried to hold back the tears rising in my eyes.

"What was your favorite part?" Jimmy asked.

"Of what?" my mother asked

I felt my heart sink as I sighed and closed my eyes.

"Of your day," Jimmy said.

"I got out a little bit to read in the sunshine. It's been a gorgeous day. I hope it doesn't rain. I don't like the thunder that comes with the rain."

"There's no rain in the forecast, so you should be good to go," he said.

"Thanks, um ..."

"Jimmy," he said. "Jimmy Sheldon."

Then they repeated the process all over again. Ogling over a wedding that never happened as the light in my mother's eyes faded and sparked. It was like trying to start a car, only for the battery to fail. In one moment, she was holding a conversation, and in the next moment, she had no idea who she was looking at.

I was thankful Jimmy was there because it was one of those days where I wasn't sure I could handle it on my own.

Chapter 9

Jimmy

I woke with Ashley in my arms for the second morning in a row. Holy shit, I could get used to that. I pulled her body close to mine, clad in nothing but one of my shirts. I pressed a small kiss to the nape of her neck and watched goosebumps rise to the surface. She groaned and stretched, her leg pressing between mine. She was the most beautiful woman on the planet in the mornings. With her auburn hair tangled up and her sleepy green eyes trying to focus. She was raw in the mornings, untainted with the stress of work. She rolled over and smiled at me, and I smoothed her hair out of her face to help her see.

"Morning, Jimmy."

"Good morning, beautiful."

"You know you don't have to call me that every morning, right?" Ashley asked.

"Fine. Good morning, gorgeous."

She giggled and shook her head, her beautiful smile encompassing her cheeks. I saw a lot of her mother in her whenever she smiled. Meeting her mother yesterday had been such a treat. I knew she was nervous about it, but I hadn't been. She had met Markus, who was more of a father to me than anything else, so it was only natural I meet her mother.

But I could see why she kept her private life away from her mother.

The topic of conversation didn't bother me. In fact, it actually gave me a few ideas for my own wedding. I could see myself eventually marrying Ashley. She was an incredible woman who warmed my soul as well as my body. Waking up to her these past two mornings had put the cherry on top of my weekend with her. I enjoyed every single moment I spent with her, and I enjoyed the intelligence and professionalism she brought to my company.

And as I gazed into her eyes that were reflecting the morning sun, my heart skipped a beat.

I was falling in love with Ashley, and I didn't want it to stop.

"Coffee?" I asked.

"Mmm, sounds wonderful," she said.

"You stay here and wake up. I'll get up and make it."

"If I could figure out how to use your fancy coffee maker, I'd make it for you."

"Or you could stay in bed and be gorgeous."

"Or you could get a pot coffee maker like everyone else," she said.

"Now what would be the fun in that?"

I made my way into the kitchen and began making coffee. I pulled out a couple of bagels, toasted them, and spread a thick layer of cream cheese around them. I heard the pitter-patter of steps coming down the hallway, and I shook my head. I knew that woman wouldn't be able to stay in bed much longer.

"Coffee and bagels? My hero," Ashley said.

"Keep talking like that and my ego might blow the windows off this place," I said.

"At least you're honest about it."

I looked over at Ashley and took her in. She'd thrown her hair up and stuck her glasses on, and she was more beautiful than I could've ever imagined. My button-down shirt hit her at her mid-thigh, taunting me with just enough of her curves to get my engines roaring. Her legs were smooth, and the sleeves were rolled up so she could use her hands. My shirt was baggy as hell on her, and she wore it with a pride I basked in.

"Coffee with cream and sugar for you, and a toasted everything bagel with cream cheese."

"Hope you have a spare toothbrush I can borrow," Ashley said.

"Don't worry. My guest bathroom is full of things you can use to clean up," I said.

"Do you have plans for the day?"

"Nope. Sunday's the one day I take off from the company. Unless an emergency takes place, it's my day to do as I wish."

"Well, I have to go check on my puppy at the resort."

"I didn't know you had a dog."

"I haven't mentioned Chipper?"

"Nope."

"Awww, I'm a terrible puppy owner. Yeah. I got him about a week or so ago. He's a beagle puppy," she said.

"I take it this resort you speak of is a place for him to go and play with other dogs?"

"It's lots of things. They groom him and feed him, and yeah, he gets to play with other dogs. He gets pampered while he's there, and it makes me feel less guilty that he's there while I'm at work," she said.

"I'd like to meet this puppy sometime," I said.

"Well, once I move into my new place, we could stay there one night, and you can meet him."

"When are you moving, by the way?"

"The end of next week. Saturday, actually."

"I want to be there to help," I said.

"You don't have to do that, Jimmy."

"Well, I'm going to, so there. What time?" I asked.

"Ten in the morning, but there are people helping me on the other end."

"So what time do you need me and where?"

"Eight o'clock at my place?"

"Are you sure?" I asked.

"You're a dick?"

"Possibly?"

She giggled over her coffee mug as my phone rang out into the apartment. I rolled my eyes and got up from my seat, reluctant to leave the beauty of Ashley behind. But when I saw it was Markus calling, I got excited.

"Hey, hey, hey, Markus. What's up?" I asked.

"I take it you've already had your coffee," he said.

"In the process, yes," I said.

"Is that Markus?" Ashley asked.

"It is."

"Hi, Markus!"

"You tell that beautiful woman I said hello," Markus said.

"Markus says you're beautiful and hello," I said. "So, to what do I owe this morning phone call?"

"I wanna take you out to lunch."

"I'm there," I said. "Just tell me when and where."

"Toro Toro? Around noon?"

"You want to eat at Toro Toro?" I asked.

"Hell, yeah, I do. I love that place. I don't have to spend a hundred bucks on lunch when I can get great food there for thirty."

"Toro Toro it is. I'll see you then."

"Sounds like a date," Ashley said with a grin.

"I figured with you needing to go check on your puppy, I could get some lunch with Markus."

"You don't have to pass anything by me. I get it. He's important to you. Even if I didn't have something to do, I wouldn't want you to feel like you had to turn it down."

"You're amazing, you know that?"

I bent down to kiss her cheek before I went to get ready. I could hear Ashley cleaning up in the guest bathroom, and a part of me wanted her to come in here with me, to stand at the empty sink next to me and get ready, to brush her teeth with me and get in the shower so I could get in behind her.

Hell, I'd miss lunch if that happened.

I took her home before heading to meet Markus. I was excited about seeing him again so soon. We had a lot to talk about, especially since he'd been gone so long.

"Took you long enough. Good thing this isn't a business meeting," Markus said.

"Good to see you too," I said.

I embraced him and patted his back before I took my seat. It had been a long time since it had been the two of us, and I was ready for whatever was going to happen. I felt like a lost son finally finding his father in the woods or some shit.

Like I'd been scared, but he was now there to provide comfort.

"I take it that pretty lady stayed with you last night."

"And the night before," I said.

"I like her. You keep her. Otherwise, I'll swoop in and claim her," Markus said.

"I don't think Jamie would like that too much."

"You have no idea the kinds of things Jamie likes," he said with a grin.

"You seem happy with her. How did you guys meet?"

"I took on a new investor, and she's his daughter."

I choked on my water as he threw his head back and laughed.

"I'm just kidding, Jimmy. We met at a bar. I was out with a couple of the guys from the board discussing some bullshit I didn't wanna talk about, and she was sitting there all alone. Went up to her, struck up a conversation, and the next minute, we were falling into bed. Over and over and over again."

"You guys got anything in common?"

"You asking because of our age difference?" he asked.

"Possibly. I want to make sure you're not getting swindled for your money," I said.

"It's nothing like that. If anything, I have to fight with her on getting her things."

"Fuck, Ashley's the same way. I can't pay for a thing in her life without it striking up some sort of discussion."

"That's how you know you got a good one, when they fight you on spending money," he said.

"To good women," Markus said.

"Here, here."

We clinked glasses as the waitress came to take our order. Markus ordered us a round of margaritas, and I rolled my eyes. It was always a party when he was in town, and I didn't know why I expected this lunch to be any different.

"How did you and Ashley meet? And don't give me this shit about work. I know you better than that," Markus said.

"I actually met her at the last party I threw for the company," I said.

"While you were still with Nina."

"Not the best look, I know, and part of it was fueled by the alcohol, sure."

"You were drinking at your own party? Must've been a hell of an accomplishment."

"It was. It was around the time we were named one of the top companies in our field worldwide," I said.

"Oh, that party. I got that invitation, by the way. But it was at the start of all this bullshit I'm having to deal with, so I wasn't free to leave my post."

"What's going on with that, by the way?" I asked.

"Fuck, don't make me go into it. I wanna enjoy my lunch before the heartburn sets in."

"Spoken like a true old man."

"You'll get there one day, and I'll be there to mock you."

"If you're still alive," I said with a grin.

"You keep pushing those buttons, Jimmy."

"You know I'm playing with you. I can hardly believe you're fifty-four. You only look thirty-four."

"I blame it on Jamie. She's got me on this skin care bullshit. Moisturizing and wrinkle creams and masks and stuff. I couldn't care less about the stuff, but she cares about a lot of my shit I know she hates."

"Aw, she wants you to stay young so she doesn't look weird standing next to you."

"She calls me 'Daddy,' you know."

"And that's enough for today," I said.

"Told you to keep pressing those buttons," Markus said.

The lunch was wonderful. We talked about nothing regarding work and talked about everything else. Ashley. Jamie. How we all met and what we all thought of everyone else. We kept poking fun at each other and drank through way too many margaritas. We had to order dessert to soak up some of the alcohol before either of us could even think about driving anywhere.

It was almost three in the afternoon before Markus went to pay.

"Nope, this one's on me," I said.

"Give me that check."

"You got dinner for all of us Friday night. I'm getting lunch."

"But you got those drinks when I came into town," he said.

"Still means it's my turn to pay. You can get the next one."

I paid the waitress, but Markus was hell-bent on leaving something. He dumped some cash onto the table on top of the tip I'd already left. I shook my head and held my arm out, waiting for him to make his way to the door. He kept stopping and talking to people like he'd known them for years, probably networking for his own business and trying to wrangle in new clients.

I'd never stop learning from that man.

"Pick up any new clients?" I asked as we headed out the door.

"Two potentials, yep. Set up some meetings with them."

"You're relentless," I said.

"And what have I always told you, Jimmy? A businessman isn't a career—"

"It's a way of life," I said.

Chapter 10

Ashley

I was glad Jimmy didn't invite me back to his place after lunch on Sunday. That meant I could get to the office early the next morning to start my investigation. Since I had gone through all the balance sheets dating back to the beginning of the company, I could start digging into the information I had. It would make it easier to approach Jimmy with all this if I already had it figured out. I had to know what was going on with his company. When I tallied up all the totals I had jotted in the margins, over twenty million dollars had been manipulated in some way over the years. Whether it was withdrawn, added without notation, or reallocated in terms of stocks, that was a lot of money being played around with.

And I needed something to take to Jimmy before I approached him with it.

I was worried about being the bearer of bad news, but I figured he would accept it well from me. Our personal relationship was good, but our working relationship was even better. He could handle it from me. Then, he'd have the reassurance that I would be there to help him every step of the way. That was the best way to approach this, given the hit he took last weekend in the media, so that was the decision I'd made.

My first stop in my investigation, however, was to the technology level of Big Steps.

I wanted to ask them how many times over the twelve-year duration of the company they had upgraded the systems we all used. And just as I figured, the systems had been upgraded many times. The guys in the department gave me access to the equations used in the Excel program for our balance sheets, so I did my due diligence. I double- and triple-checked the equations to make sure they were correct and had someone help me dig into other areas I thought could be wrong, possibly skewing the numbers like I saw them to be skewed.

But no matter where I looked, nothing was wrong with the program we were using for the balance sheets.

Then, I asked them how many times they upgraded the hardware, the actual machines our programs ran on. Apparently, they had only been upgraded once, six years ago, in fact. And the reason for their upgrade was that the company had taken on so many clients, the hardware could no longer keep up with the software requirements the technology department needed. I asked to see the original order form if they still had it, and I saw on the sheet where both Jimmy and Ross had signed off on it.

So, nothing was wrong with the technology behind the balance sheets.

I thanked them for their time and went back to my office. The only other conclusion I had was that someone was manipulating the money, and we weren't catching it. I kept looking through all the accounts associated with the toggled currency, and I couldn't seem to find a trace of anything. The account numbers were solid, and no nameless accounts had been created. There were no ghost accounts or ones that had been shut down out of nowhere, but there was a set of initials that kept popping up from time to time.

L.R.

The initials weren't attached to the creation of any accounts, but they were attached to the deposits and withdrawals that had been manipulated over the course of time. For every transaction recorded in Big Steps, there had to be an identification number and a username submitted to process the transaction. The problem was, I didn't recognize the initials, and that was even more unusual because I'd become very familiar with all of them during my time in accounting.

A username was never a simple pair of initials. It was usually a first name, a middle initial, and a last name or some sort of combination that could easily point back to the person who initiated the transaction. It was to help follow where money was allocated throughout the company. There were certain accountants who dealt with specific budgets for the other departments in the company. It was usually easy to determine where withdrawals and deposits were coming from based on the username handling the transaction.

However, I didn't know who these initials belonged to. I couldn't recall any time in the four years I had been with Big Steps that anyone had used "L.R." as their username. Maybe it meant left-right? Not a username but a set of buttons that had been touched in order to initiate the transaction? Or maybe it was someone who used to work at the company and still had access to things?

All I knew was the initials were attached to every transaction that had been mishandled, and those initials went all the way back to the inception of the company.

Well, it sort of went back to start of the company.

The first three years of the balance sheets didn't have the initials L.R. on them. There were still mishandled transactions, but the username portion of the transaction information was simply blank, which wasn't odd necessarily. The company was in its infancy, and the software was new. People probably assumed it was Jimmy trying to do something or Ross trying to familiarize himself with how everything worked, but I knew better than that.

I pulled up a log of all past and present company employees on my computer and jotted down everyone with those initials. Then, I went back through and jotted down everyone who had the initials "R.L." Just to be sure. But none of those people made any sense. One of them had worked in Human Resources for two years, another one had been a personal assistant to Ross for six months, and the other one was the four-year-old daughter of someone who worked in the IT department.

There was, however, a nagging sensation in the back of my mind.

When Nina had caught us kissing in Jimmy's office a couple of weeks ago, she made an explicit statement that he would pay for what he'd done to her. She stormed out in a huff, and Jimmy tried to settle me down, but I knew she was a woman who would make good on her word. The initials didn't seem to line up with Nina, but I had problems shaking the idea it might've been her behind the discrepancies. I didn't know how those dots were going to fall into place or how those lines were going to connect those dots, but something in the pit of my gut was tugging me in that direction.

And that wasn't good.

The company was finally getting over the fiasco with Jimmy's social media. His Public Relations department was still trying to get his reputation in a decent place. His lawyers still didn't know who made the threat or where it had come from. What we all knew was that it had caused so much turmoil and distress, the public was now in an uproar. The lawyers were working as fast as they could so Jimmy could make good on his word and seem confident to the public, but the further they dug into the accusation, the more lost they became.

Kind of like I was with these balance sheets.

All I knew was that I needed more time than what I spent in the office. I needed more time to dig into this without the possibility of Jimmy hovering over my shoulder. Whether this was tied to Nina or not.

So I stuffed the balance sheets into my bag and headed for his office.

"Jimmy?"

"Good morning, Ashley. What can I do for you?"

"Would it be possible for me to have the day off?" I asked.

"Has something happened with your mother again?"

I didn't want to lie. I didn't have to have to look him in the face and lie to him about what was happening, but this was my responsibility. At least it had been when Mr. Brent threw those balance sheets back down on my desk. That was the first stop I needed to make. I needed to ask that man why he felt the need to pass these things off to me even though I'd been promoted.

"I wanted to go see her, yes. The nursing home called, and she's a little disoriented. Ornery. They're hoping I can calm her down before they medically intervene."

"Then what are you still doing here? I'll come with you," Jimmy said.

"If it's okay with you, I think I need to do this on my own. If she doesn't remember you, it might only agitate her more. Sometimes, having me there during these spells makes things worse, but sometimes, it makes it better. If she doesn't even remember meeting you ..."

"It's okay. Whatever you need. Take the day and let me know how she's doing, okay? Promise?"

I felt my stomach fall to my toes as I looked into his eyes full of sympathy and understanding and a desire to help. I felt terrible. I felt like I was hiding something from him, but with his reputation on the mend and his hunt for his accuser still taking place, the last thing I wanted to do was flood his world with more stuff to worry about.

I could take care of this on my own. After all, my initiative is what got me this job.

"I promise," I said. "I'll call you soon."

Chapter 11

Jimmy

My Tuesday morning was filled with a massive investors meeting. Everyone wanted to meet to see how things were going to go this next quarter, especially with the hit the company's image was taking in the press. I had to reassure them that their money was going to see profit and that they were not only investing in a strong company but also a strong man. I still had my wedding ring on to communicate commitment, and I had Ashley in the corner ready to rock and roll with numbers.

But what really gave me a piece of mind was Markus.

He would be the one to get them all back on track.

The meeting went smoothly, and Ashley did a fantastic job. She fielded all their questions and ran calculations in her head on the spot. She really was a force to be reckoned with, and Markus kept shooting me looks. I knew those looks.

They were looks of pride and envy, all rolled into one.

"That was a hell of a parlor trick Ashley pulled."

Markus shut the door behind him as we walked into my office.

"I'm telling you, she's my new secret weapon," I said.

"Was she really doing all of that on the spot?" he asked.

"She was. And she speed-reads. She devoured the entire US tax code in a few days. Saved me millions this year."

"She up for hire?" he asked.

"Not a fucking chance," I said with a grin. "I'm glad you were at that meeting today, though. I wasn't sure how it was going to go."

"I wasn't sure either. Figured I'd finally drop by to one of those things, but you handled yourself well. You were direct and to the point and honest with your answers, even if the answer wasn't what they wanted."

"I still don't know what's taking my lawyers so long to find this."

"For all you know, it was some asshole on the internet being stupid and making a joke that spun out of control. That's the problem with all this technology. It links us, but it gives idiots a platform to spew stupid shit all the time," he said.

"Well, I'm making good on my word. When my lawyers figure out who did this, I'll be serving them with papers."

"And what if it's some crusty little bitch in his momma's basement?"

"Then I'll scare him. People need to know that their words come with weight. They can destroy things easily and all at the click of a few buttons."

"I'm with you if you're serious about it," he said.

"Thanks."

"Oh, are you free for dinner tonight? You can bring Jamie too. I was thinking of taking Ross out, but I figured Ashley would like to get out for a bit too."

"Everything okay?"

"She struggles with her mother. Alzheimer's."

"Shit, I know how that is," he said.

"You do?" I asked.

"Hell, yeah. I don't talk about it or anything, but my mother had Alzheimer's. It's a shit show, especially in the later years. You know how long her mother's had it?"

"Fix or six years, I think?"

"Damn. That's rough. You're giving her time off if she needs it, right?"

"That's why she was gone most of the day yesterday," I said.

"Good. Because her mother doesn't have much time left. But yeah, I'll come on out to dinner. My treat, though. You paid this past weekend."

"I know, I know. And I don't go back on my word. Though, I wish we could do this more often."

"Well, you might get your wish."

"What do you mean?" I asked.

"I'm fielding all that shit with my company, and it's not looking good. I mean, it is looking good, but it'll look better if I'm down here with it. So I might end up back on this side of the country."

"You're shitting me."

"Nope. You know I got my main set up in Miami. Headquarters is in Alberta, but my main office that fields all types of shit is right here."

"You're moving back?" I asked.

"Don't get too excited or start drawing up announcements. Nothing's set in stone. If I can resolve the issues and stay in Canada, I will. But the more I meet with the idiots I employed, the more it's looking like I might have to move out here for a spell."

"Markus, I hate that your company's struggling like that, but I can't help but be excited at the idea that you might be coming back."

"I know, I know. I was in meetings about it all day yesterday. Figured a meeting at another company would lift my spirits apparently."

"Let me get a few things done around here, and then we can all go for dinner," I said.

Markus stuck around, meandering to all the departments and talking people up. Jamie came up to the top floor around four thirty and greeted him with a kiss. I caught Ashley's stare from her office, and I could see the light in her eyes. She watched the two of them embrace in the hallway, and the smile that crossed her face filled my heart with joy.

I wanted to give her that and so much more if she would let me.

All of us headed out to dinner again, and it was wonderful, but it didn't stay that way for long. I followed Markus's eyesight as we sat down and watched his face fall immediately.

And there was only one person on the planet who could suck the life out of him that quickly.

"Jimmy, can we go somewhere else?" Ashley asked.

I turned around and saw Nina, her eyes hooked on the table.

"It'll be fine," Markus said.

"We've got this," I said.

"I'll handle it if she says anything," Markus said. "You've had enough of a presence in the media for one year."

I heard Nina's heels clicking over to the table, that light little sound that always sent the worst of shivers down my spine. I could feel her gaze on me as Ashley slipped her hand into mine, her arm trembling. I hated that she felt like this. I hated that I couldn't escape this woman and that I couldn't enjoy a fucking dinner out without Nina popped up and ruining all this shit.

How did she have the money to be here, anyway?

"Hello, gentlemen," Nina said.

"Here we go," Ross said.

"Before you say anything, I want you to know something," Markus said. "If you know what's good for you, you'll turn around and go take your seat."

"The last time I checked, I was free to walk up to whoever I wanted," Nina said.

"And that's fine, but not tonight," Markus said.

"Just go away, Nina," Ross said.

Markus shot him a look, and Ashley gripped my hand tighter. I watched Nina's eyes fall to our connection as her cheeks flushed with anger. I stared her down, letting her know she couldn't intimidate us out of here. Whatever she was looking for, she wasn't going to get tonight.

Or ever, if I had anything to do with it.

"How much is he paying you a month?" Nina asked.

"That's enough. If you couldn't handle the nature of your and Jimmy's relationship, then that's on you. But if you don't turn around and get out of here, I'll make you," Markus said.

"Is that a threat?" Nina asked.

"Might be. I'd think it was more a promise, though," he said. "Either way, you ready to find out? Because I've been waiting a long time to put you where you belong."

I looked over at Ashley, and I saw her eyes in her lap, shamed into a position she should never be in. I reached over and crooked my finger underneath her chin and lifted her head. Her eyes were filled with fear. Worry. Apprehension. What was supposed to be a lovely dinner had quickly become another fiasco because of Nina.

I was ready to take out a restraining order on the woman.

"You'll pay."

I whipped my head up to Nina as Markus stepped in between us.

"Time to go," he said.

"You'll pay, Jimmy Sheldon. And if you don't think you will, then think again," Nina said.

"I need a manager, please," Markus said. "Someone to get this wild animal out from underneath our feet."

There was a commotion as a couple of people came over and took Nina by her arms. She tried to shake them off, stumbling in her heels as her hair flew everywhere. I shook my head as Markus stuck with her, making sure the two people could handle her flailing body all the way out the door. I felt Ashley's forehead come down on my shoulder, and then a small sniffle hit my ear.

She was crying.

I had wanted to take us all out for a nice dinner, and now the love of my life was crying.

Chapter 12

Ashley

I couldn't get what Nina said out of my head. She had been right there in the middle of a restaurant spouting the same threat she had when she'd seen Jimmy and me in his office. In front of all sorts of people who probably overheard her. The moment kept running through my mind. How Markus had to step in and how Ross was tired of her antics. We all were. We were all tired of Nina popping up out of nowhere and causing issues with everything.

Something had to be done about Nina.

Something drastic.

If she kept up this bullshit, it was only going to cause more issues, and not just with Jimmy and me but his company as well. I was more than convinced she was behind all this stuff going on. The balance sheet issues and the "anonymous accusation" of Jimmy bribing people to favor his product. It had "vengeful sort-of ex" written all over it.

If she had the money to continue frequenting places like that, then who knows what else she was capable of getting her hands on.

I sat at my desk all day with my nose in some work. I had a full day of individual conference calls with all the investors. They were demanding them while Jimmy settled his public persona, which meant I got to rattle off twenty-one separate times that things were okay at the company, that their money was safe and would gross them the exact net profit I had projected for them over the next quarter. They really were a handful, and I could see how a career could be made from simply running behind these man-children.

But I was good at doing it, so I kept my nose to the grind.

"Ashley?"

"Hmm?"

I lifted my head from the paperwork on my desk and saw Jimmy standing at the door.

"Hey there."

"Hi," I said.

"How did all those conference calls go today?" Jimmy asked.

"About as good and monotonous as you could expect. But they're done, and I'm simply completing some paperwork to have on file about them."

"Are you free for dinner tonight?"

"I kind of want to go home and hang out with Chipper."

"Are you sure? I've got a very relaxing evening planned for us," he said.

"Jimmy, I have a home I can go to and a dog I need to take care of. I can't run off with you after every day simply because you want to hang out."

I knew how sharp it sounded the moment it came flying out of my mouth. I sighed and closed my eyes and then leaned back in my chair. Jimmy came in and shut the door behind him, turning his "boss mode" off. His eyes became compassionate, and his movements became gentler. He walked around my desk and sat on the edge of it, his hands shoved into his pockets and his eyes dancing around my face.

"Chipper's more than welcome at my place," he said.

"I know," I said with a sigh.

"You really could use a relaxing evening."

"We tried that yesterday, remember?" I asked.

"In," he said. "A relaxing evening in. I've got dinner ready to cook at my place, and a full-body massage is waiting for you."

"Man, that sounds good," I said.

"Then say 'yes.' Let me cook for you. We can pop open a bottle of wine, settle down after a long day. I'll get you relaxed with a full-body massage, and maybe we can share a bath together."

"And where is Chipper in this equation?"

"With Cass?" he asked.

"If she didn't love that puppy so much, I'd say you were trying to tell me to get rid of my puppy for the evening."

"Like I said, he's welcome if you want to bring him. I'll cook him up some rice and shred some chicken up for him."

"You'd do that for me? Aw, Jimmy. So sweet," I said with a wink.

"So, dinner in? At my place?" he asked.

"Let me call Cass and make sure she can take Chipper. If she can, no worries. She's got a key. If she can't, I'll have to go pick him up."

"Perfect. Now, what's on your mind?"

"Hmm?"

"What's got you so locked up?" he asked. "Do you want to talk about it? Is it your mother?"

I felt that same pang of guilt rush through my body as I shook my head.

"It's not my mother. And it's really nothing. This Nina thing is getting out of control is all."

"I agree with you on that, and I'm working on a plan. Right now, all we can do is know that the city is on our side. Her antics in public won't be tolerated in places I frequent, so stick by my side and you'll be okay."

"The first time it was 'oh, you're good. No need to worry.' Now, I'm having to stick by your side to stay safe from her?" I asked.

"I promise you, Markus and I are in the process of fixing all this. We aren't going to live like this. Nina isn't going to continue kicking up dust the way she is, not if I have anything to do with it."

I wanted to believe him, but a part of me couldn't. For every good thing in my life, there was always a bad. There was always a karmic balance that took place, no matter what. And Jimmy was too much of a good thing, which meant there was too much of a bad thing I'd always have to put up with in order to stay with him.

It was how things worked, and nothing more.

"Let me call Cass and see what she's up to. Then, we can go from there," I said.

"I'll be in my office waiting for you," Jimmy said.

Cass was more than willing to take Chipper, and a part of me was relieved at that. The more I thought about it, the more a night in with Jimmy sounded like the perfect answer to my worries. I left my car in the parking garage and left in Jimmy's car, watching the world pass us by. His hand was cradling mine, and I could feel his pulse throbbing against my wrist faster and faster the closer we got to his apartment.

I was still in awe of how he could cook. The honey and basil-coated chicken smelled delicious, and the garlic green beans were as fresh as it got. I was tasked with picking out a bottle of white wine for us to share, so I popped it open and poured each of us a glass. It was nice, eating in with Jimmy and getting into a routine and getting comfortable as I gazed at him from across his little eating nook.

"Why don't you have a formal dining room?" I asked.

"One couldn't fit in this kitchen," Jimmy said.

"You've got space, even for a simple table that seats four."

"Do you not like the nook?"

"It's a bit small. Do you not usually have company over? Friends? Markus? Anything like that?"

"Not where meals are concerned. I've never led the kind of life that gave me the ability to take pride in family dinners. If I'm not wining and dining a client, it's me eating here alone. No point in a big table if it's just me. Plus, the view from the nook is outstanding."

"Maybe one day you'll have a reason to get a formal dining table," I said.

His eyes locked with mine as he took a bite of his chicken.

"Maybe I will," he said.

Dinner was wonderful, and I was insistent on washing the dishes. We polished off the bottle of wine as I stacked everything in the dishwasher, and Jimmy turned it on so we could get out of there. We settled on the couch, and he started his massage, working his way up my calf and digging his hands into my skin.

"Oh, you weren't joking," I said.

"I never joke when it comes to touching you."

"Oh, that feels—oh. So good."

"If you turn over, I'll massage your back," he said.

Up and up he went, his hands digging lightly into my strained muscles. The tension in my lower back melted, and the boulder on my shoulders slowly rolled off. Thoughts of the balance sheets and Nina and my mother's problems melted away, and all I was focused on was the motions of his hands, how delicate his touch was and how firm his palms felt against my skin. My nipples were rising to painful peaks, and I could feel his cock pressing against my ass. His lips dipped to my ear, caressing the shell before he pressed a kiss to my skin.

"If you remove your clothes, I could give you a more thorough massage."

The two of us were undressed in a matter of minutes. His hands ran along my sides before he picked me up into his arms. My head was swimming with the wine, and my stomach was warm with the dinner he'd cooked for me. He tossed me onto the bed as giggles spilled from my lips. His cock was thick and ready for my body, and my thighs were aching to have him between them.

He wasted no time in giving me what I wanted.

Our lips collided as his hand slipped behind my neck. My hips rolled into him as he sank between my legs. I wrapped my thighs around him and locked my ankles as the tip of his dick teased my dripping pussy. I was breathing his air, feeling his back twitch underneath my fingers as my hands rushed down his back.

He slid into me effortlessly. He pushed my walls back, making my entire body shudder. My lips kissed his neck, nipped at his pulse point, and grazed along his shoulder. His face was buried into my neck, peppering me with kisses and lapping at the dip in my shoulder.

"You're beautiful, Ashley. So beautiful."

"Go faster. Harder. Please, Jimmy. Make me forget."

He pounded into my hips, my hands curling into his hair. I couldn't get enough of him, of his muscles contracting against my skin and his sweat dripping on my body. His lips kept devouring me, wrapping around my nipples and sucking them until they burned. His cock slid deep into my body, shooting electricity through my veins and setting the tips of my toes on fire. His hands found mine and pinned them over my head, interlocking our fingers as he found my gaze.

He held my stare, his hips rolling deeply as my feet dug into his backside.

Thrust for thrust, I met him with my body. He kissed my chest and licked my neck and left bite marks I knew I would find in the morning. My body hummed for him. Shook for him. Jumped at his touch and gave into his undulations. My toes ran up and down the backs of his thighs, pulling goosebumps onto his skin and sending a shiver down his spine.

I captured his lips, my throat swallowing his groans.

My pussy lips folded to him and exposed my clit to his curls. The fire that burned in my gut raged throughout my entire body. My hands gripped his and my heels dug into the mattress. I pressed my body deeper, arching into him to find any friction I could. I felt his smile as he kissed me over and over until my lips were nothing but swollen, throbbing pillows. My body was covered in a sheen of sweat, desire dripping from my pores as my toes began to curl.

"Yes. Just like this. Keep going. Jimmy, keep going!"

I slammed my hips into him, and it threw me over the edge. I moaned out into his room, my cries filling the corners of his penthouse apartment. The skyline of Miami backdropped my body, his curtains open for the world to look in on us. I could feel my pussy clenching him tightly, milking him for the come my throbbing walls were greedy for.

"Ashley. Shit. You make me feel ... oh, fuck."

He grunted and groaned, his knees scraping along the mattress for traction. His hands released mine, sliding down my arms and cupping my breasts. He fell into me, holding himself up with his forearms as his cock twitched against my walls. I could feel his threads of come painting me, marking me as his own once again like he had so many times before.

He collapsed on top of me, our intermingled arousal dripping from between my legs.

My lips found his jawline, kissing it endlessly until he could turn and capture my lips.

"Now I'm all sweaty," I said breathlessly.

"I've got an idea for that, if you give me a second," Jimmy said.

"Take all the seconds you need. I love you like this."

"Like what?" he asked.

"Blanketing me with your strength. It's a comforting feeling like you ground me or something."

I felt him smiling into my skin as he placed a kiss on my breast. He helped me up as he moved, my body limp against his. The room was tilting, and my head was dizzy from the orgasm that shot through my body. I could feel our wetness pooling underneath my legs, but I was soon being lifted into the air away from the mattress and suspended against the rock-hard body of a man I was growing to adore.

Growing to love, if I was honest with myself.

"I told you there was a bath in store at some point in time," Jimmy said. "Guess we could make it a bubble bath."

He carried me into his decadent bathroom as the carved marble jet tub stared back at me.

"Are you going to join me?" I asked.

He set me in the tub before he turned on the water.

"Is that really a question?" he asked.

He toggled the spouts until the water was the right temperature. It was warm and soothing to my skin, relieving my muscles of the tension they still held from our encounter. Jimmy poured bubbles into it, the smell of lemon and roses rising from the water. I sighed and closed my eyes, feeling Jimmy lift me up so he could get behind my body.

Then, he cradled me in his arms, guarding me against any worry trying to get to me from the outside.

"Do you need anything?" Jimmy asked.

"I should be asking you that question," I said. "This entire night's been for me."

"Not just for you. Your presence has been for me. Enjoying your body was for me. Being in this bath with you was for me."

"And here I thought you were busting out the big guns."

"Trust me, if you have to question it, then it's not 'the big guns.' "

"I hear that ego talking again," I said.

"Only because you make me want to flex it."

"I have no idea if that's a compliment or something I should be afraid of."

"You make me want to be better in all the things I do. I'd say that's a hell of a compliment."

"Well, you make me want to fall asleep on you, so don't mind me if I start snoring."

"Trusting me with your body in its most vulnerable state? There's no greater compliment you could pay me," he said.

I smiled as I curled into him, feeling his strong arms wrap around me. I curled my knees up and sat between his legs as the water continued to fill up the tub. The jets kicked in, creating more bubbles and more relaxation as Jimmy stretched out his leg. His foot turned off the spouts as the jets pummeled our bodies, massaging us as the two of us sat together, wet and spent in each other's arms.

It was official.

I could really get used to a life like this.

Chapter 13

Jimmy

Riding to work with Ashley was a thrill in and of itself. Holding her hand as we pulled into the place I had built with my own two hands felt natural. Freeing. Like the way my life should've always been. She leaned over and gave me a kiss before we got out of my car, and the two of us stepped into the elevator to head up to our offices.

I walked her to her office, my hand trying not to lead her by the small of her back. I knew how important it was for her to not have any shows of affection in the office, and I understood. She didn't want to be seen as the woman who slept her way to the top.

I didn't want that for her, either.

"Thanks for last night," Ashley said. "I really enjoyed it."

"Thank you for staying with me," I said. "I like waking up to you."

The blush that tinted her cheeks tugged at my cock.

"But, it's time to get to work," I said.

"Unfortunately," she said with a sigh.

"Have you finished those balance sheets yet?"

A look of panic washed over her face as I grinned.

"I know everything that goes on in my company. I know Mr. Brent gave them to you to look over. I wasn't happy with him, but he gave a sound reason for it. He said you were looking them over before you got promoted, and he didn't trust anyone else with them. You should take it as a compliment."

"After he grabbed me in the elevator, I'll hold off on the celebration. I'm sorry if you felt like I was keeping it from you or something."

"Nope. Very little gets under my nose at this company. How much longer do you need on them?" I asked.

Her hesitation made me uncomfortable before she answered.

"I'm not sure. You know me. I want to triple-check my own work before I hand it over," she said.

She seemed nervous, but we hadn't had time to stop for coffee. Maybe she was simply tired? If it were any other employee, I would've gotten the impression they were lying to me, but I knew Ashley wouldn't do something like that. We had an honest relationship in and out of the office. Maybe she thought I was still upset for her taking on those balance sheets. And for the most part, I wasn't. There was a part of me that felt as if Mr. Brent was taking advantage of her kindness, but he did provide a sound argument for why he wanted her looking at them and no one else.

"I promise I'm not upset. I had a stern talk with Mr. Brent about utilizing you further, but don't think I'm upset with you taking on that work," I said.

"I know," Ashley said. "I know. And thank you. I guess I better start learning how to say no."

"Uh-huh," I said. "Well, not to me I hope."

"You're bad."

"Only for you, Miss Ternbeau."

"Mr. Sheldon?"

Ashley's office door flew open without a knock, and the head of my security was standing in the doorway.

"Yes?" I asked.

"I need to see you in your office. Now."

"I'll be there in a second," I said.

"Is everything okay?" Ashley asked.

"Don't worry about anything. You get those balance sheets finished up and get them to me."

"Yes, sir," she said with a grin.

I followed the head of security into my office, and he shut the door promptly behind him. There was a worry etched on his face that made

BUILDING BILLIONS - PART 2

me sick to my stomach. I leaned against my desk and unbuttoned my coat, trying to give myself room to breathe.

Whatever it was, it wasn't going to be good.

"What's going on, Masser?"

"We caught someone early this morning breaking in and going through files downstairs."

"What?" I asked.

"Yeah. The guy had a bunch of matches and gasoline on him, too, in a bag he had thrown over his shoulder."

"Are you fucking kidding me?"

"Not in the least. One of my men caught him rifling through things, and they were able to subdue him, but we're having to reroute people into the side entrance because he dumped some gasoline on things."

"Shit. Is he still here?" I asked. "Was anything damaged?"

"Some carpeting in the file room and some of the files will need to be burned and reprinted, but it wasn't bad. No fires were started, but it was clear that was his intent."

"Is he still here?"

"We have him in custody, yes."

"I wanna see him. Now."

I followed Masser down to the main level of my headquarters, and the smell of gasoline was pungent. People were murmuring and whispering, trying to figure out what was going in. I felt my blood boiling as Masser led me into his office.

And there sat a weaselly little bum with stringy hair and beady eyes and terribly bad breath.

"Who are you?" I asked.

But the man stayed silent.

"You can answer my questions, or I can turn you over to federal authorities."

"You're not that important," the man said.

"Wanna test that theory?" I asked. "Who are you?"

"No, thanks," he said.

"What were you doing breaking into my building?"

"You need better security. Your men here are weak."

"And yet here you sit. Why did you douse my file room in gasoline? Enjoy watching things go up in flames?" I asked.

"Go to hell."

"I'll pay you ten thousand dollars to answer my questions, and I won't even turn you over to the authorities."

"Sir, I don't think that's—"

I held up my hand to Masser in order to shut him up.

"She paid me double that," the man said.

I felt the hairs on the back of my neck stand on end. I knew exactly who he was talking about. I looked over at Masser, and he reached over, pressing the red button next to his bookcase. His entire office was wired for two reasons. He could either make it soundproof or he could make it one big ass microphone.

And this asshole was about to be recorded.

"Forty thousand dollars," I said.

"And no police?"

"I'll involve the police if I see fit," I said. "I don't know you, and you clearly don't look like the type of customer I would take on. So who sent you? Who hired you?"

"No, thanks. I'll take my chances with the cops," he said.

"Will the cops give you forty thousand dollars?" I asked.

"You can't buy love, Jimmy. Love is stronger than that."

I threw my head back and laughed. Holy fuck. This man had no idea Nina was using him. I could hear sirens outside as footsteps came rumbling down the hallway. The man started to panic, his beady eyes widening and his lip quivering in fear.

She was fucking good, but I was even better.

"Open up. Police."

"Let them in, Masser," I said.

"Okay, okay, okay. I'll tell you. It was Nina. Nina Black. She hired me for twenty thousand dollars to come in and burn up your files. She even told me where they were. She bribed the guard at the back door to let me in this morning. Please. Please let me go. I won't even take the money."

"Love, huh? Must not be a very strong bond," I said.

The police ripped him up from the chair as Masser turned off the recording.

"Get us a copy of that, would you?" the officer asked.

"I'll make sure Masser gets it to you," I said.

The man was struggling against the police, and they had to subdue him. He kept yelling about how he had kept his deal and how he expected to see the money he was owed, but I had no intention of paying him. It wasn't until the police were in that room that he fessed up. He didn't sell Nina out to me.

He confessed in front of the cops in a fit of fear.

"I'll have my secretary contact someone to come clean up the mess in the file room. Throw open windows and pull some fans up from the basement. We need to get the smell of gasoline out of this building."

"Already on it, sir," Masser said.

I headed back up to my office, and Ashley was fidgeting at my door. She turned to me, her eyes wide as the sun, and I could tell she knew something was wrong. She was fighting every urge to run to me, throw her arms around me, and bury herself against my body. I quickly opened my office door and let her in, and the moment it closed, her arms were around me.

"It's okay. It's fine. It's all taken care of," I said.

"It was Nina, wasn't it?" she asked. "I was right."

"Nina is going to jail for a very long time for all of this," I said.

"What happened?"

"She hired a guy to come in and burn up my file room downstairs. Bribed my security guard at the back door to get in. I need to have a talk with him, but I'm pretty sure today will be his last day at work."

"I told you she was dangerous, Jimmy. I told you we needed to watch out for her."

"And now, it's finished. The confession's on tape, the police have hauled the guy off, and soon, they'll be looking to arrest Nina for a host of things that will keep her in jail for a long time to come. You don't have to worry about her anymore."

I could feel Ashley's shoulders moving with her sobs. It hurt my heart that she had been so frightened during all of this. I should've kept her closer and made her feel safer in her environment. I had underestimated the anger Nina possessed, and I'd put Ashley in the line of fire because of it. That wasn't going to happen again. I was no longer underestimating the people around me, not when I had so much to lose.

"This is all too much," Ashley said breathlessly.

I held her out from my chest and wiped her tears away with my thumbs.

"Everything is done. It's all gone. Nina's never coming back once they arrest her," I said.

"You don't know that. You've told me twice now that she's no longer an issue, and look what's happened."

"The police weren't involved before, but they are now. Nina can't hide. She's not capable of it. She needs to be tended to. She needs to stand out and be noticed."

The tears falling from Ashley's eyes were sad, but her face was angry. The light behind her eyes was fiery. She pulled away from me and turned her back, shaking her head as if she couldn't believe the situation.

"Ashley."

"I'm taking the day off," she said.

"If that's what you need, that's fine. You can take one of my—"

"I need to be alone," she said.

"If you're still this scared, then you shouldn't be."

"If you had listened to me the first time, then it wouldn't have escalated. Why didn't you listen to me, Jimmy?"

She was pleading with me, asking me for answers when I had none. I felt helpless to stop her emotional tirade. I felt helpless to reassure her that this was over and that Nina was gone.

"I'm sorry," I said.

"I'm taking the day off. I'll take the balance sheets with me, and I'll get it done," she said.

"Whatever you need, you know I'll support it."

"You always do."

She walked out of my office and stormed into hers. I watched as she shoved papers into her bag, and it seemed like a lot for a few balance sheets. She threw her bag over her shoulder and raced back by me, not bothering to look as she headed for the elevator.

Everything inside of me wanted to go after her, keep her company, and show her I wasn't going to leave her alone like this. But I understood that she needed space, time to breathe after the fast pace of the past couple of months.

I watched the elevator door close on her, her eyes cast to her feet as tears dripped from her cheeks.

Fuck. How the hell was I going to fix this?

Chapter 14

Ashley

I was riding the wave of still being upset with Jimmy. I called work and told Jimmy I was taking an emotional day to myself. He didn't seem happy about it, but he also didn't question it. Of course, the real reason was that I wanted to get to the bottom of this L.R. thing.

I wanted to be able to finish my research before I moved into my new apartment.

"Did someone order pizza?"

I smiled as I got off the couch when Chipper wagged his tail at the door.

"You're a sight for sore eyes," I said.

"Tomorrow's the big move-in day. You ready?" Cass asked.

"Yep. Everything's packed. Just getting some last-minute work done."

"Lots of numbers stuff I don't care about?" she asked.

"I think you'll care about this."

"Oh, something juicy. Let Chipper and me curl up so we can listen."

"Okay, so. I've been taking a look at some balance sheets, and I've been finding a lot of issues."

"What kinds of issues?"

"A lot of money is being toggled, deposited where it shouldn't be and withdrawn when it needs to be somewhere else. It's all very small amounts, and the numbers get fudged to be right on the balance sheets. The end figure is right, but the numbers added and subtracted to get there don't add up."

"Oh, shit. Someone's taking money from the company?" she asked.

"Not exactly. It's really hard to follow at times, but it looks like some money's taken right out, and some money is invested in stock options. Or at least dumped into that account. Some money's even added, and it's all in small chunks that aren't tallied in the final figure on the sheet."

"Someone's giving the company money?"

"All I know is about twenty million dollars' worth of money has been played around with for at least the past nine years, but I think it's been happening since the beginning of the company."

"Why do you say that?"

"Every transaction is paired with a username linking an accountant to the transaction. Certain accountants, among their other jobs, handle the budgets and accounts for certain departments in the company. Having a username there makes it easy to see who toggled the money and if it was placed in the right spot."

"Because of what accounts they control. Got it."

"Right. But usernames are usually a mixture of a first name, middle initial, and last name. Or some form that makes it easy to identify the person," I said.

"Okay?"

"The weird transactions only have initials. L.R."

"Not the format of usernames you guys use, I take it."

"No. Not at all. I went through all the company logs to see who had the initials L.R. or R.L., and none of them make sense," I said.

"Have you told Jimmy?"

"This is technically my responsibility, so I want all the answers before I go to him. Do you have some free time today?"

"I'm off today," Cass said. "I closed down to give myself a day to breathe."

"Wanna come to the library with me and do some research?"

"I'm not sure what you think you'll find, and I think you're crazy for not telling Jimmy, but sure. Sounds like fun."

Our trip to the library was fruitless. I wasn't sure what I was expecting to find, but there was nothing. There were articles about Jimmy when he first started the company, and I looked to see if anyone was mentioned with those initials. I found public records of all the paperwork that went into starting Big Steps, and no one signed anything with the initials L.R. I was frustrated and left with dead ends and had all of these loose ends I had no idea how to tie together.

"You really need to tell him," Cass said.

"But if I can't find these answers, he's going to think I'm incapable of doing my job," I said.

"He didn't hire you to be a detective, Ash. He hired you to be an accountant. You've done the accounting work. Now let him to the rest of it. Or whoever he has to do the rest of it."

"I got this job because I took initiative."

"And now you look like an idiot. You're chasing all these dead ends hoping to solve some big mystery when it could all be a big misunderstanding. Did you ever think this might be a software issue?"

"I already talked with the tech department. I checked the equations in the spreadsheet application myself. They're all correct. The coding is correct. The hardware's only been changed out once, and that was to accommodate the load of clients Jimmy took on six years ago."

"Shit. You really dug into this."

"I really did, but I want solid proof. Jimmy is still recovering his image from that stuff in the media, and this would be a massive blow," I said.

"Did he ever figure out who made the accusation? That shit was everywhere for days."

"No, but he has a feeling about who it was. Hopefully, that issue was resolved today, but I don't want to talk about it in case he's trying to keep it under wraps."

"That's fine. I can respect that. Though I'll secretly try to pry it out of you later," she said.

"Duly noted. I want everything before I go to him. He can't handle another blow like this."

"I think you're underestimating him a bit, don't you think?"

But before I could answer Cass's question, my phone rang in my purse.

"Hello?"

"Hey there."

"Jimmy. Hi."

Cass gave me a wry little grin as I sat back in my chair.

"I know you're taking the day, but I thought maybe drinks tonight might cheer you up," he said.

"Drinks with Markus, I take it?"

"Yes. Drinks with Markus. Is that okay?"

"Of course, it is," I said. "I got some sleep and did some more work on these balance sheets, and I feel a little better. Not much, but I'm getting there."

"I know these past couple of months have been a whirlwind for you, but I want you to know I'm here for you. I get it. Things can get tough, but everything is okay now."

I felt my stomach drop at his words.

"Yeah. For now," I said.

"Come get drinks. It'll make you feel better. Pick you up at seven?"

"I'll see you then."

"Am I on doggy duty tonight again?" Cass asked.

"Could you?"

"Of course. I love that little guy," she said.

"Thank you so much."

"But you should tell him. If you want to pay me, then pay me that way. Tell Jimmy what's going on with his company. It's his company, Ashley."

"Okay. I hear you. I'll tell him. Once I can get moved. Yikes."

"We are so throwing a massive party at your new place," she said.

I gave Ocean Homes a call to confirm my move-in time for tomorrow. I was stacking boxes near the front door, making sure things could go smoothly in the morning. I tidied myself up a bit for drinks, picked out a nice dress, and decided to let my hair down for the evening.

I slapped on some makeup, slipped into a pair of heels, and waited for Jimmy to pick me up.

The drive over was silent but tense. I gripped Jimmy's hand harder than I'd intended, and I could tell he was studying me. I felt beads of nervous sweat sliding down my back as my eyes gazed out the window.

I wasn't sure I'd be able to get through this weekend without telling him about what I'd found.

"Ashley. You look lovely as ever," Markus said.

"You're way too kind. Thank you," I said.

The two of us embraced before Jimmy enveloped Markus in a hug.

"I hear Nina finally got what she deserved," Markus said.

"Nina was arrested around four this afternoon," Jimmy said.

"Well, that's a relief," I said.

"Good riddance too. That woman is nothing but trouble in heels," Markus said.

"So, in celebration of having her out of our lives, we're going to talk about anything else," Jimmy said. "After I get back from the bathroom."

I watched Jimmy get up from the booth, and he planted a kiss on my cheek. His touch was warm and inviting, and it settled the last of my nerves. I watched him walk away as a glass of wine was set in front of me, and I found Markus eyeing me curiously.

"You make him happy, you know."

"He makes me happy too. I just hate that he has to put up with my anxiety sometimes," I said.

"Jimmy's the perfect man for someone like you. Never feel like you're weighing him down."

"I'll try not to. Where's Jamie tonight?"

"She had a spa day and then came back to the hotel and crashed. Must be hard getting massages and pedicures. I've been dragging her around to so many things that I didn't have the heart to wake her up."

"You're a good man, Markus. She's lucky to have you."

"And I'm lucky to have her. I'm a hard man who's rarely romantic, and I don't know why she puts up with me."

"Because you probably aren't as rough with her as you think you are," I said.

"I wouldn't be too sure of that," he said with a wink.

"And that's why you and Jimmy get along. You're both bad."

"To the bone," he said.

"Does your family live in Canada?" I asked. "That's where you're from, right?"

"No. I'm from right here in Miami. Self-made man here. But when I got my company off the ground, I hit some roadblocks, and it made me establish some outposts in Canada. My headquarters is in Alberta."

"Do you like it there?"

"I do. So does my mother, when she can remember it."

"What do you mean?" I asked.

"My mother has Alzheimer's. I took her with me to keep her comfortable and keep her close to family. I'm all she's got, and she doesn't have much time anyway."

"I'm so sorry. And can completely relate. My mother has Alzheimer's too."

"How far along is she in it?" he asked.

"Six years. It's pretty advanced. I just had to sign off on bumping her treatment up a bit."

"Those are rough days. I had to do it with my mother a few months ago. She's almost at a point where medication and therapy don't help."

"Does she have any lucid moments?"

"If you're looking for reassurance, I've got none. She barely knows who I am now. It's hard, the hardest thing I've ever had to do. But I know when she does finally pass, she'll be relieved of the hell her own mind put her in."

I felt my eyes watering as I looked down into my wine glass.

"Don't get mad at him, but Jimmy did mention it to me. He said your mom was having a bad day one day, and it sort of slipped. I wanted you to know that if you need someone who gets it, I get it. Jimmy's a good supporter, but he doesn't get it. And sometimes, you need someone who understands."

"I'm not upset. You're like a father to Jimmy. I figured he's probably told you a lot," I said.

"Does she ever call you other people's names?" he asked.

"No, but she does keep insisting I introduce her to my husband. She's hell-bent on the fact that I got married."

"The last time I visited my mother, she called me Lou, which was close. That's my middle name. My father's name was Lou, and I figured she thought maybe I was him."

"Do you look a lot like your father?" I asked.

"People think that. I don't see it, but we never want to see our parents in us when we age."

"Age. Like you're old or something," I said with a grin.

"I feel old sometimes."

"I bet Jamie doesn't think that. Does correcting your mother ever make her upset?"

"All the time now. It used to not be like that, but this last time, I corrected her out of an automatic reaction, and she spiraled."

"I'm so sorry," I said.

"Jimmy tells me he met your mother. How did that go?"

"Um, about as good as you could expect. She automatically assumed he was my husband and went on and on about our wedding. I was mortified until Jimmy started playing along."

"He's a good man like that. He's encountered my mother a few times, so it wasn't his first time with something like this."

"She didn't even get through the conversation before she forgot who he was."

"I'm sorry," he said.

"It's not a big deal. I mean it is, but I'm used to it. Jimmy took it well, and it doesn't seem to have made him scream and run for the hills, so that's a good thing."

"Can I ask you a question?"

"Sure."

"Is your father still alive?"

"He's not. Car accident took him a few years back."

"Does your mother ever think he's still alive?"

"Worse. She sometimes forgets she even got married. The nurses will come in and call her by her name, and she'll correct them, tell them her last name is Roth and not Bryant."

"How do you deal with that? How does it not break you?" I asked.

"I might drink a little too much for my own good sometimes. I talk with Jamie about it a lot. But mostly, it comes with times. As harsh as it sounds, you do get used to it. You have to. It'll crumble you otherwise."

"It really doesn't get easier, does it?" I asked.

"No. But know that you can call me anytime you want if you want to talk about it. If talking to Jimmy or your friends don't work, get my number from Jimmy. He'll understand."

"Thanks, Markus. I appreciate it."

"Did the toilet swallow that man whole?" Markus asked.

"Nope. I saw you were already finished with your drink and decided to get you another one."

I looked up at Jimmy and saw him steadying the drinks in his hands. I reached up for the glass of wine he got for me, so it wouldn't spill. Then, he handed Markus his drink. Jimmy's touch on my back was comforting. Reassuring. And sitting at the table with someone who understood what I was going through relaxed me in a way I couldn't describe.

"To a bright future and a better life," Jimmy said.

"Here, here," Markus said.

Then the three of us clinked our glasses, settled back into our chairs, and laughed until our stomachs ached.

Chapter 15

Jimmy

I woke up with Ashley's body entangled with mine, and I sighed. Every morning I got to wake up to her warmth next to me was a blessing. I looked down into her face as her cheek squished into my shoulder, and my heart rate sped up.

I was in love with this woman.

I only wished she would tell me what was bothering her.

I knew something was there. She had been tense all last night. The car ride to the bar had been silent and uncomfortable. I wanted to know what was wrong. I wanted to know how I could make it better. I wanted her to stop pushing me away and let me in like I'd allowed her in.

I wanted the chance to prove to her that I could support her through anything, no matter how big it seemed to her.

I didn't want Nina getting in the way of this. I didn't want her ruining yet another good thing in my life. Nina was gone, and she wasn't coming back. I only needed to find a way to convince Ashley of that.

"Why are you staring at me?"

"Good morning to you too," I said.

"What time is it?" Ashley asked.

"Seven thirty," I said. "You ready for the big move?"

"Crap. I'm already late."

Ashley threw the covers off her, but I pulled her back to bed. My lips descended to her neck and I began kissing her, listening to soft moans fall from her lips.

"Jimmy, I need coffee," she said.

"Oh, I've got a better way to wake you up."

"Then I'll have to shower."

"We can shower at your new place."

"Jimmy, I need—oh, right there."

I grinned against her breast, teasing her nipple with my tongue as her hips rolled into me.

She was warm and wet, percolating with the thought of my cock taking her. I pushed my shirt up her body, moved her panties to the side, and slid my throbbing cock into her pussy. She was beautiful. Her eyes were hazy with sleep, but her face was scrunched with pleasure. I thrust into her slowly, waking her up as her body became more alert.

Her skin flushed, and her hands crept up my arms. She pulled me down to her, our lips intertwining. Even in the morning, she tasted phenomenal like wine and toast and a hint of butter. I threaded our fingers together and pinned her hands above her head. Her toes sent shivers up the backs of my legs. Her pussy was fluttering. Pulsing. Dripping on my skin as my lips nipped at her pulse point.

"Come for me," I said in a whisper. "I know you want to."

"Jimmy. Oh, Jimmy. So good. Oh ... you feel—"

Her sentiment was cut off by the intensity of her orgasm. Her jaw unhinged as her body shook, and I could feel her pussy pulling me deeper. Her toes curled into my calves when my cock exploded, filling her with my come while her nails curled into my hands.

I settled onto her body, cherishing the moment with her, feeling her soft warmth against my aching muscles.

"Mmm, what a good morning," she said.

"And I plan to have many more of them."

I slid from between her legs and helped her to her feet. The two of us got cleaned up, and we had just enough time to get coffee. The moving van I had ordered for her was sitting in front of her complex, and men were standing at her apartment door as she eyed me carefully.

"Just the two of us, huh?"

"You've got help on one end, but I figured you could use some help on this end. Come on. Let's get you moved in," I said.

We sat on the edge of her couch as we watched the movers stack the truck. She kept looking over at me and giggling, and the sound was wonderful. We sipped our coffee and kept moving around, trying to stay out of the way as Ashley called out commands.

"Yep, let's take that now."

"Nope, do that last."

"That goes to the curb. I'm not taking that with me."

"Be careful with that box. It's got glass in it."

We drove over to her new place where a host of other men were waiting to unload her things. It was the first time I was seeing where she was moving, and the look of pride on her face was worth it. Between the guys the complex had and the guys I hired, it only took them three trips to get everything upstairs.

She didn't have much, but she was proud of what she had.

I loved that about her.

"You have a beautiful view of Miami," I said.

"And I'm close to the beach."

"Want to take a walk?"

"I really should start unpacking."

"We can do that tonight. I'll help you with it all. Take a walk with me. Let's go break in the sand."

I held my hand out for her, and she smiled up at me. Those sparkling green eyes and that red hair piled high on her head had me bewitched. I couldn't resist that smile of hers. It melted my heart every time she flashed it. We set our empty coffee cups on the edge of her new kitchen counter, and the two of us made our way downstairs.

Four blocks later, we were standing on the beach.

We walked hand in hand, carrying our shoes as the waves flooded over our feet. The more we walked, the more Ashley leaned into me, relaxing and casting her worries away. Maybe the stress of the move to a new place was what had been bothering her. I wrapped my arm around her and kissed the top of her head, enjoying the sound of the ocean with the woman I had come to love.

"Thank you," she said.

"For what?"

"For hiring those movers. For that van. For getting me out on this walk."

"I'm here to help," I said.

"You're here for more than that. I want you to know I appreciate you, and I care about you. Everything I do is because of that."

I looked down at her as the two of us stopped walking.

"I care about you, too, Ashley. A great deal. I want you to know you can rely on me. I'll always listen, and I'll always try to help whenever I can. You can come to me. Always."

"I know," she said. "Thank you, Jimmy."

The waves crept across our feet as I raised my hand to her cheek. I ran my thumb along her skin, taking in the softness of her features. I got lost in her eyes, writing books about her beauty inside my head. I guided her face to mine, savoring the taste of her lips as we connected. The sun was hanging high in the sky, and the seagulls were singing off in the distance. She stood on her tiptoes, wrapped her arms around my neck, and I bent her backward to taste more of her and feel her body arch into mine.

I could've stayed like that forever. I could've held her in my arms with the sun on our backs and been the happiest man alive. If my company went under the next day, I would still be okay because I knew Ashley would be there to help me stay afloat.

"I'm the luckiest man alive," I said against her lips.

"Then come here and give the luckiest girl alive another kiss."

Chapter 16

Ashley

Jimmy and I spent the rest of the day on the beach before heading to my place to unpack. He helped me get all the big furniture where it needed to be before we headed back to his place. I knew unpacking was going to be a process, and I didn't want it to stress me out any more than it already had.

Plus, I wanted to wake up in Jimmy's arms again.

I looked up into his face and was wracked with guilt. I needed to tell him and soon. I was no closer to finding out who was behind all this stuff with his balance sheets, and someone would catch what was going on. If I wasn't the one to tell him, then he would think I'd been hiding something from him. And I didn't want him to think that when I was trying to help him.

Jimmy was still asleep at ten o'clock when I got a call from the nursing home. I slipped from his arms and picked up my phone, and I could hear my mother on the other end. I put my clothes on as fast as I could and placed a chaste kiss on Jimmy's cheek.

I hated leaving him to wake up alone, but my mother needed me.

I sent him a text message as I raced down to the lobby. I hailed a cab that took me straight to the nursing home. I ran into the complex and raced down the hallway, my knotted hair billowing behind me.

"Mom? Mom, where are you?"

I found her and the nurses in the common room, struggling to get her to stand up. She was spitting in their faces and trying to kick at them, and the scene was too much for me to take. I pushed one of the nurses out of the way and got down on my knees, trying to still my mother's movements. If she wasn't careful, she was going to hurt herself again.

"Mom. Look at me. Mom."

"Get off me!" she said.

"Stop fighting them, and they will," I said.

My mother's eyes connected with mine, but I could tell she didn't recognize me. Her hair was wild, her arms were trembling, and I motioned for the nurses to back off. I knew they were trying to do what was best for her, but I was beginning to question their ability to take care of my mother. Every time I came into this facility, they were either trying to control her movements or trying to sedate her with something.

And I was getting tired of it.

"Where's Ashley? Where's my daughter? She'll know what to do."

I tried to choke back my tears as I slid my purse to the floor.

"Ashley sent me," I said. "She's moving into a new place today, but she didn't want you to be alone."

"Moving? Why the hell is she moving? She's only a child. Get me out of here. I need to go see my daughter now."

"I promise you, she's going to come see you soon, and she's going to take you on a tour of her new apartment. She's so proud of it. The room she has set up for you has the best view."

"It really does," said a deep, masculine voice.

I felt the hairs on the back of my neck stand on end. I slowly turned around, my eyes taking Jimmy in, his long legs clad only in jeans. The simple white shirt he had on was tight around his chest, and his arms were traced with veins as he clenched his fists in his pockets.

"Who the hell is that?" my mother asked.

"Jimmy," he said. "Jimmy Sheldon. I'm a friend of your daughter's."

He came and stood behind me, his warmth comforting me as I tried to take my mother's hands.

But she wrenched them away before I could hold her.

"We need to get you back to your room. You know everyone here loves you," I said.

"Then why are they trying to poke me with needles? Ashley knows I hate needles."

"Probably because you're spitting at them," I said.

"They were trying to make me move. I don't want to move."

"Where were they trying to make you move?" I asked.

"The kitchen, but I'm not hungry."

I looked over at one of the nurses as I rose to my feet.

"She hasn't been eating well," the nurse said. "She'll ask for something and then forgets she asked for it. Sometimes, she'll get hungry and then forget she's hungry."

"Is that even possible?" I asked.

"When it's this advanced, yes. With Alzheimer's, it's never the disease that hurts them. It's the forgetting of basic things that does," the nurse said.

"Where in the world is the breakfast I ordered?" my mother asked. "I told these people I was hungry an hour ago."

"Then why don't we go to the kitchen and get you settled in for a meal, huh?" I asked.

I watched Jimmy offer his hand to my mother, and he helped her up from her chair. He offered his arm, and she took it, a smile beaming across her face. The two of them walked arm-in-arm to the kitchen, the nurses guiding them along their way.

But the moment was short-lived.

"Why are we in the kitchen?" my mother asked.

"You said you were hungry," Jimmy said. "Would you like to eat breakfast with me?"

"I'm not hungry. I want to go sit in the sun. It's a beautiful day today," my mother said.

"Will you sit with me while I eat?" Jimmy asked.

"Why would I want to sit and watch a man eat?" my mother said. "My life doesn't revolve around you, Leonard. When are you going to learn that?"

My eyes widened at the sound of my father's name as a tear rushed down my cheek.

"I'm sorry. I didn't mean to assume," Jimmy said.

"Sorry? Who are you? Leonard never apologizes."

My mother pulled away from Jimmy, and I stepped up to the plate.

"Why don't we go lie down?" I asked. "Watch a movie? Read a book?"

But my mother shoved me away so hard, she fell backward.

"Mom!"

"I am not your mother! Get away from me!"

She began flailing and crying, and I felt Jimmy's hands come down around my upper arms. The nurses rushed to my mother, checking to make sure she hadn't hurt herself. I looked over at one of the nurses as my mother continued to fight, kicking at the people trying to help her off the floor.

I saw the needle in her hand, and I nodded, giving her permission to do the one thing my mother would hate me for doing to her.

"Leave me alone! Get away from me! You are not sticking me with that."

I put my face in my hands as they helped my mother into a wheelchair. Jimmy's arms were around my waist, his lips pressing kisses into the top of my head. I was shaking, sobbing, no longer trying to cover up the pain I was in.

"Come here," Jimmy said. "I'm right here."

I sobbed into his shirt. I fisted it with all my might as rivers of tears flowed down my face. He scooted me to a little alcove off to the side and held me as tightly as he could. Kiss after kiss was placed on top of my head. His hands stroked through my knotted hair as I sniffled into his chest.

"Jimmy. I'm sor—"

"Don't even," he said. "Don't finish that statement."

"I should've—"

"I'm here, and that's all that matters. You texted me. You told me what was going on, and I'm here. As I should be," he said.

"What am I going to do?" I asked.

He rocked me side to side, swaying me in the small closet we were cooped up in as people passed us by. I wrapped my arms around his waist and pushed my hands underneath his shirt, feeling the strength of his lower back and trying to draw from it.

"I think a day in with your best friend might help," Jimmy said. "Why don't you call her and invite her over to your new place? I'll order you guys some pizza, the two of you can unpack, and I'll come by later tonight with dinner."

"That actually sounds nice," I said.

"Give her a call. I'll get the pizza ordered, and I'll take you back to your place."

"Okay," I said. "Okay. Yeah. That sounds good."

Cass met me at Ocean Homes, and I ran into her arms. She kept shushing me in my ear as Jimmy held the pizza beside us. He walked us up to my new place, set the pizza on the counter, and gave me one last kiss before he left.

"Fuck, that man is gorgeous," she said.

"Seriously?" I asked.

"What? I can comment. I just can't touch. So, what happened with your mom?"

"Everything this time. She kept asking for me but didn't recognize me. She kept forgetting she was hungry and had ordered food. She thought Jimmy was my father. It was a mess. She spiraled. She pushed me away. I had to give the nurses permission for them to medicate her so they could get her back to her room."

Cass pulled me to her again as my body started to shake.

"Your new place looks nice," she said.

"Thanks."

"And that pizza smells good."

"It does."

"Why don't we eat and then go room by room, unpack, and talk?"

"That's fine with me. I just want to sit down," I said.

We carried the pizza over to the couch and sat looking out over the expanse of Miami. It really was a beautiful view, and it was calming to sit in the light of the sun. I chewed on the pepperoni pizza as Cass held my hand, comforting me as we sat in silence.

"Now, I'm going to bug you about this because you're calm, and Jimmy was here."

"No, I haven't told him yet," I said.

"You need to, Ashley."

"One issue at a time. My mother just melted down."

"And now that issue has been resolved, at least for now," she said.

"I don't know if I'll ever figure out who's doing all of this."

"Not your job. You've done your job, and now, your job is to tell Jimmy what you've found," she said.

"I know. I hear you, and I'm going to tell him. Can we just get through today first?"

"If you promise me you'll tell him tomorrow."

"Cass."

"Look, people get fired over less. And if you don't want to look like you've fucked your way into corporate, then you need to conduct this as if you aren't trying to protect your boyfriend."

"I'm not trying to protect him."

"Yes, you are. You said so yourself. You don't think he can handle another blow like this because of the PR crap in the media or whatever. But if you weren't screwing around with him, if you didn't care about him, would you be waiting this long to tell him? Would you be trying to figure out who this was?"

"Fuck," I said breathlessly.

"It's okay to want to protect him, but if you keep this from him and he finds out and he still keeps you around, he's not doing it because you're good at your job. He's doing it because you two are an item. Talk to him, Ashley. Tell him you've done your job, and this is what you've found. Like you would do if the two of you weren't together."

"Okay," I said. "I promise I'll tell him tomorrow."

"Good. Now, we're going to finish this pizza because it's awesome. Then, we're going to start in your bathroom and work our way across the apartment. By the time we're done today, your new apartment will be ready."

"You're going to make me haul all the cardboard boxes to the trash compactor, aren't you?" I asked.

"Only because I'll have to hang all the pictures. I love you, but you can't hang a picture to save your life."

Chapter 17

Jimmy

"Jimmy?"

I looked up from my desk and saw Ashley standing there with her red hair piled high on her head and her glasses sliding down her nose. No matter what she wore and no matter what day it was, she never ceased to take my breath away. She had on this flowing summer dress with matching flats and a cardigan thrown over her shoulders. But there was something in her eyes that made me nervous.

"What is it, Ashley?"

"There's something I need to talk with you about," she said.

"Sure. Come in and sit down."

She stepped in and closed the door, her shoulders hunched over a bit. Nerves began bubbling in my stomach as I stood up from my chair. Was she okay? Had something happened with her mother? She turned back around and started for the chair in front of my desk, her fingers twirling in her cardigan. She was chewing on her lower lip, and her eyes were darting around the room. It was the first time Ashley had ever looked fearfully uncomfortable in my office.

Holy hell, was she about to break up with me?

I started panicking. I sat on the edge of my desk and tried to keep my cool, but inside, I was freaking out. If Nina had ruined this for me, I would never forgive her. I would come down on her with a fury and light her ass up. And if for some ungodly reason, Nina had pulled something to stress Ashley out from beyond her holding cell, I would make sure that woman never saw the light of day again. She didn't get to ruin my life because she got too greedy with my money. She didn't get to ruin the best thing to ever happen to me because I'd ended our arrangement.

That wasn't how this worked.

"Ashley, you're worrying me. What's wrong?" I asked.

"I need to talk with you about these," she said.

She dipped into the bag around her shoulders and pulled out some files. The manila folders had the balance sheets hanging out of them, and I could see they were all marked up. She sat down in the chair and handed them to me, my arm stretching out for the files.

Was this all she wanted to talk about? Why was it making her so nervous?

"You finished them," I said.

"I did, but it took me awhile because of all the discrepancies."

"Discrepancies?" I asked.

"Take a look."

Her fingers were still fiddling with her cardigan as I put the folders on my desk. I picked one up and began to flip through it, my eyes scanning all the notes. There were arrows and plus signs and minus signs and numbers. Words like "stocks and bonds" and "withdrawals" and a bunch of circles around the letters L.R. I furrowed my brow as I flipped through the pages, taking in how many notes Ashley had made in the margins.

"What is all this?" I asked.

"These balance sheets are from the past couple of years at the company."

"It looks like a whole lot more," I said.

"I printed them all out in a bunch larger print so I could be sure of the numbers."

"There are a lot of notes here. No wonder it took you so long."

"And I went back all the way to the start of the company."

I rose my eyes to Ashley and quirked an eyebrow. She had printed off all the balance sheets since the inception of the company twelve years ago?

"Why?" I asked.

"Because the discrepancies are everywhere. Back before you promoted me, Mr. Brent had me going through all this stuff. I figured there was an issue with the algorithm in the Excel spreadsheet, so I made a note of it and sent it back."

"But then he brought them to you again," I said.

"Yes. With a note telling me there was nothing wrong with the Excel spreadsheet. So I kept digging and kept making notations, and they go all the way back, Jimmy. There are small amounts of money transferred into random stock accounts and small amounts withdrawn too. Other amounts that come out of nowhere are put into those stock accounts before they disappear. The total of any one transaction never breaches fifty dollars, and the totals at the end of the balance sheets are correct. But the actual numbers used to get to that total are wrong. I notated everything on the sheets."

"I see that," I said.

"I know it looks confusing, but if you tally all of it up, over twenty million dollars have been toggled."

I almost swallowed my tongue at the number.

"What?" I asked.

"The only connection I can find are the initials L.R. It's attached to most of the transactions."

"Not all of them?" I asked.

"No. The first three years of the company don't have usernames attached to the transactions, but after that, L.R. starts popping up. I tried tracking the person down, trying to figure out who it could be. It was why it took me so long. I'm sorry, Jimmy."

"No need to be sorry," I said as I picked up another file.

"I went down to the tech department and looked through everything. The hardware's only been updated once, and both you and Ross signed off on it. I checked all the algorithms in the software myself, and nothing was wrong. It's not the technology, Jimmy. Someone's messing with the company's money."

"This was the source of your stress over the past week, wasn't it?" I asked.

I watched Ashley look down into her lap as I sighed.

"Ashley, I'm not upset with you."

"I tried figuring out who L.R. could be, but none of what I found made sense. I figured it might've been Nina, but nothing links back to her in any way. Then, I pulled up the past and present company logs, and no one with the initials L.R. or R.L. make any sense. One worked for HR two years ago, one was Ross's personal assistant for a few months, and the other is a child of someone in the Public Relations department."

"You did all of that over this past week," I said.

"I also have to apologize to you," she said.

"Why?"

"Remember when I told you something was wrong with my mother?" she asked.

I watched her heave a heavy sigh as I grinned.

"Your mother was fine, wasn't she?"

"I needed an excuse to do a little more digging. I took the balance sheets home with me and finished off the tallies. I didn't want to worry you because this is a job I technically started before I was promoted, and I got this position because of my initiative, and with everything that happened in the press a couple of weeks ago—"

I set the folder on the desk and pushed myself away from it. I took Ashley's hand in mine, silencing her cute little ramble. I pulled her up to her feet, wrapped my arm around her, and pulled her to me for a gentle kiss. Her hands settled on my hips as I held her closely, allowing my tongue to swipe out and touch her lips. The way she groaned into me, melting into my embrace, it sent my mind spiraling.

"You're remarkable," I said.

"I'm sorry for lying to you and keeping this from you," Ashley said.

"As far as I'm concerned, you were doing your job. Thank you for bringing this to my attention."

"Do you have any idea who L.R. could be? It's not a username I recognize from anyone in the Accounting department over the past four years."

"I have no idea. I have some things I could take a look at myself, but nothing immediately comes to mind."

"Do you think Ross might know?"

"You could ask him, but I doubt it."

I looked down into Ashley's big green eyes, but my nerves weren't abating. Twenty million dollars was a serious amount of money. I had to figure out where the hell that money was going. I had to figure out who the fuck was stealing from my company. I understood why Nina was Ashley's first suspect, but if this had been going on for years, Nina wasn't a possibility. She'd only been in my life for two years, and though she was a conniving bitch, she wasn't smart enough to orchestrate something like this.

My gut reaction was that it was someone on the inside, but who the hell had I employed for that long?

"I'll talk to Ross and see if he can think of anyone off the top of his head. You get back to work," I said.

"Jimmy, I should've come to you wish this sooner. I'm sorry," Ashley said.

"As your boss, I have to reprimand you. Yes, you should've come to me the moment you realized these discrepancies weren't technological or formulaic. I appreciate you taking the initiative, but I didn't hire you to be a detective. I hired you to be the investor's accountant."

"Yes, sir."

"As your significant other? Thank you for putting in all that work. I appreciate you being concerned about how this would affect me. I'll take this to Ross. Now let me make some phone calls," I said.

I dismissed Ashley from my office and watched her walk back into hers. She seemed to stand a little taller, and her hands were no longer twisted up in her cardigan. That was enough for me right now. I had greater things to tend to if I was going to continue spending my evenings with her, however, which meant I had to redirect.

"Knock, knock." Ross poked his head into my office.

"Just the man I wanted to see. Get in here," I said.

"Everything okay? Things seemed pretty tense in here with you and Ashley," he said.

"Do the initials L.R. mean anything to you?" I asked.

"Uh, left-right?"

"A person's initials?" I asked.

"Lionel Richie?"

"Come on, Ross. Be serious."

"What's this about?" he asked.

"Twenty million dollars, that's what."

"I'm not following."

"Remember me reprimanding Mr. Brent for slapping those balance sheets on Ashley's desk a few days ago?"

"What's going on, Jimmy?"

"She found some issues she says date all the way back to the beginning of the company."

I picked up a folder and handed it to Ross for him to look at. The moment he flipped it open, his eyes grew wide. He was taking in all of Ashley's notes and running the calculations in his head. He flipped sheet after sheet, his hands gripping the folder so hard, his knuckles were turning white.

"Holy shit."

"Yeah. Ashley said the initials L.R. are attached to just about every one of the faulty transactions too," I said.

"We need to check employee records," Ross said.

"She already did that. Past and present."

"Is it possible this is Nina?"

"Not if it dates back more than a couple of years."

"Jimmy, this is serious."

"You think I don't know that?" I asked. "None of the transactions breaches fifty dollars at a time, and the ending totals for the balance sheets are what they're supposed to be, according to Ashley. It would be easy for someone to overlook that, especially with all the work we throw at our Accounting department."

"That's still no excuse. You mean to tell me no one caught this in the twelve years we've been active?" he asked.

"I don't know. Ross, I don't fucking know. I've got a couple of places I could look to make sense of the initials, but that's literally all I have at my disposal without involving the police."

"I'm sure the IT department can help us out with this. We have a cybersecurity department for a reason, Jimmy. I'll go down there and see what I can figure out."

"Thanks. I've got some more employee records I can scour," I said.

"Meet back here at the end of the day?" he asked.

"See you then."

Chapter 18

Ashley

I could breathe a little easier now that I'd told Jimmy about what I found. Cass had been right. Telling him even though I didn't have any answers was what I needed to do, not only for the company but for the sake of my sanity. With that off my shoulders, I could focus on other things like setting up the rest of my new place and making sure my mother was okay.

Her last episode had me worried. Her lucidity was fading, and it was becoming almost impossible for the nurses at the home to treat her without constant medical intervention. She was growing angry and becoming combative. She was forgetting she was hungry and missing meals. I used the time I wasn't unpacking my apartment to do research and figure out where I could go from here with my mother and what the best course of action was. If the nursing home she was in didn't have the ability to take care of her, that was fine. They had taken care of her for the past three years, and they had done a wonderful job.

Maybe it was time for me to find her a new place.

Sitting down at my desk, I tried to focus on the PDF I was creating for the investors, but my mind kept going back to those balance sheets. I wish Jimmy would've let me talk to Ross, not because I could've communicated the message better but because I wanted to get a read on his body language. I didn't think Jimmy would steal from his company but approaching him gave me the ability to study him. To gauge his reaction to the situation and figure out where he stood with it. I was able to scrutinize him without him knowing what I was doing, which went a long way in me trying to figure out who L.R. was.

Because Jimmy wasn't going to fight this fight alone.

Being able to tell Ross would've given me the ability to scrutinize him as well. In the back of my mind, I knew Jimmy didn't have a bad bone in his body. He would never dream of stealing from his company. But owners and operators did that sort of thing and so did COOs.

I didn't want to think Ross was capable of something like that, but no one ever knew until it happened.

In situations like these, it always seemed to be the person least suspected of doing it.

I sent off the quarterly PDF to the investors before Ross came and knocked on my door. Jimmy was holding a meeting in his office to go over the possibilities of who L.R. could be. I gathered my things and locked up my office, suddenly paranoid about anyone going in there while something like this was happening.

When I walked into Jimmy's office, I could tell he was distressed.

"Ross, shut my door," Jimmy said. "We can sit in the corner on the couches."

"Jimmy, what's going on?" I asked.

"Doors shut," Ross said.

"You're worrying me," I said.

"Ross went and talked to the IT department yesterday. He was able to pull up the past few months of faulty transactions and trace the IP address. Someone's tapping into our system from outside this company," Jimmy said.

"And you have proof of that," I said.

"Yes," Ross said. "IT is sending us a full workup this afternoon. I wanted them to give us IP addresses and trace them back as far as they could pull up the original transactions."

"So, we aren't looking at someone in the company?" I asked.

"Not necessarily," Jimmy said. "But with the tampering coming from the outside, it's going to force us to involve the police."

"Which means more media attention if someone talks," Ross said.

"So make them sign an NDA or something," I said.

BUILDING BILLIONS - PART 2

"The police don't work like that," Jimmy said.

"Hire a private detective. A security team. Something," I said. "Jimmy, if this gets out to the public—"

"I know, I know," Jimmy said. "I know, Ashley, but I don't have a lot of choices here. If this was coming from inside the company, tracking the person down would be easy. I don't have the tools or the resources to track down who this could be outside of these walls."

"Then pay someone, Jimmy. That's your resource," I said.

"Told you she wouldn't be a fan," Ross said.

A knock came at the door before the knob began to turn. I watched Jimmy's face morph from confusion to anger until the door slowly opened. Jimmy breathed a sigh of relief as Markus walked through the doors, and I was glad he was there.

Maybe he could talk some sense into Jimmy.

"Everything good?" Markus asked.

"We're just ... having a meeting," Jimmy said.

"Anything I can help with?" Markus asked.

"Actually, yes," I said.

"Jimmy? You want to loop him in?" Ross asked.

"Loop me in on what?" Markus asked.

"Just hold off on your lecture until later," Jimmy said.

"I'm all ears, then," Markus said.

"Someone's been stealing and tampering with company money," Jimmy said.

"What?" Markus asked.

"Ashley was the one who caught the figures. The balance sheets dating close to the inception of the company all have weird little transactions. The entire balance sheet for any given month has been tampered with," Jimmy said.

"I don't follow," Markus said.

"Someone's moving money around under the initials L.R.," Jimmy said. "No more than fifty dollars at a time but it's frequent. According to Ashley's totals, it's over twenty million since the start of the company."

"Basically," Ashley said. "The first three years of transactions don't have a username or initials attached to the transactions, but I'm assuming it's still the same person. Or at least the same basic action."

"Someone's stealing from my damn company, Markus, investing in stock before cashing the accounts out, going back into the balance sheets themselves, and fudging the numbers at the end of the sheets to reflect what they should. Whoever this is, they're good, but they're also not in this building."

"How do you know that?" Markus asked.

I furrowed my brow as I watched Markus's face. At first, he seemed shocked, but it was expressed by his eyebrows, not his eyes. He was studying Jimmy intently, hanging onto every word. Which would have been normal, had it not been coupled with the fidgeting Markus was doing. It was concealed, and the only reason I noticed it was because I did that kind of fidgeting all the time. Wiggling my toes in my shoes. Picking at my nails at my sides. Clenching my jaw and biting the inside of my cheek.

Markus was nervous.

"Do you have any idea who could be doing this?" Markus asked. "Because if the media gets a wind of this, you're toast."

"Thank you," I said. "Jimmy's wanting to involve the police."

"As opposed to a private team?" Markus asked.

"My thoughts exactly," I said. "What do you think he should do?"

"I think you should keep it as contained as possible until it's absolutely necessary for you to involve outside forces, whether it's a private team or the Miami PD," Markus said.

"Markus? Do you have any idea who L.R. might be?" I asked.

"What's L.R.?" he asked.

"The initials that keep popping up with the transactions," Jimmy said.

"Not off the top of my head. If you're looking at someone from the outside like you think, it could literally be anyone," Markus said.

"No one at all? From the investor board or anyone from the parties we threw together?" Jimmy asked.

"I told you I don't know," Markus said.

I looked over at Ross as I drew in a deep breath. Defensiveness. Markus was getting defensive at our questions. Why? Did he feel he was being interrogated? Ross looked at me with a weird stare before we turned our gazes to Jimmy, but his back was to us, and he was looking out the window. His hand was raking through his hair, and his leg was jiggling. His shoulders pulled taut, he heaved a heavy sigh.

"I'll do what I can to help, but if you really want my advice? Keep it contained," Markus said. "For as long as you can."

Markus's statement sat with me all night. Why would someone who cared so much about Jimmy not want him to take whatever measures necessary to figure out what was happening? Keeping it within the company seemed idiotic, especially when they had proof the transactions were happening from outside the company. I sat in my apartment that night and racked my brain. I knew I was missing something obvious, something vital.

I closed my eyes and finished off my glass of wine. Jimmy had dismissed me early from that meeting but kept Markus and Ross with him. Part of me was irritated that he wanted me gone, but part of me saw it as a good thing. I was able to come home, relax, and try to see if I could figure out what it was I felt I was missing.

I brought my wine glass to my lips as I rifled through my memories of Markus.

Then, it hit me.

The conversation I'd had with Markus last weekend.

"The last time I visited my mother, she called me Lou. Which was close. That's my middle name. My father's name was Lou, and I figured she thought maybe I was him."

My skin crawled as I continued to recount the conversation in my mind.

"Worse. She sometimes forgets she even got married. The nurses will come in and call her by her name, and she'll correct them, tell them her last name is Roth and not Bryant."

Was it possible? Was I reaching too far for this? Jimmy had told me on several occasions Markus had been in this with him from the beginning as his very first investor. That would've given Markus access to all sorts of things, especially if Jimmy had leaned on him for financial and business advice. Hell, Jimmy might've given Markus access to his accounts to help him grow his company in the beginning. And Jimmy would be blind to it. He trusted Markus like a son trusted his father, which meant the last person he would consider would be Markus.

In situations like these, it always seemed to be the person least suspected of doing it.

I shot up from the couch and set my wine on the coffee table. I couldn't believe I was just figuring this out. I had to tell Jimmy. I had no idea how I was going to tell Jimmy, but it was the only thing that made sense. With Markus being there from the beginning and having his set-up in Alberta, it would make sense as to why the transactions were coming from outside the company. And if "Lou Roth" was the reason for choosing the initials L.R., it meant there was only one last question to ask.

When had Markus moved to Alberta from Miami?

Because I bet if I asked Jimmy, he would say nine years or so, which would be three years after his company was started.

Chapter 19

Jimmy

"Jimmy Sheldon."

"Morning, Jimmy," Ashley said.

"Good morning, beautiful. To what do I owe this phone call? Are you in your office already?"

"No, that's what I was calling about. I'm not really feeling well."

"Are you okay?" I asked.

"Yeah, I think so. I mean, I need to book a doctor's appointment. My doctor has walk-in hours this morning. I've just had this nagging migraine, and nothing I have around here is helping."

"Then stay there. I'll come get you and take you to the doctor."

"It's fine. Really. I'm going to take a cab. I wanted to call and let you know I probably won't be in until after lunch."

"Take the day. Or know you have the option. You can always remote into work with the laptop we gave you if you need to," I said.

"I always forget I have that thing."

"Are you sure you don't need me to come take you? It's been a slow morning."

"I promise I'm okay. I think I need something stronger to get it to go away. Or maybe I should stop drinking so much coffee."

"I'd hate to see the caffeine withdrawals."

"I blame you. The stuff at your place is much more potent than what I usually drink," she said.

"You seem to be in high spirits for someone with a migraine."

"Sunglasses and a dark room do wonders," she said.

"Well, get yourself to a doctor and call me to let me know what's going on. Okay? And don't come in here with a migraine. Stay home if you need to."

"Thanks, Jimmy."

I hung up the phone and sat back in my chair. I wanted to believe Ashley, but there had been moments recently when she had openly admitted to lying to me. I understood the reasons, and she had come clean about all of it, but I still couldn't shake the feeling she wasn't actually sick. Was she still worried about this money business? I mean, it had us all worried. But she did her job beautifully. She didn't have to worry about it any longer. This wasn't an issue she needed to deal with anymore.

Was she lying to me again? Or was she really sick?

I sat back in my chair and turned to look out over the Miami ocean. The options I had to tackle this issue were rolling around in my head. I agreed with Markus about keeping this as contained as possible, but not involving anyone seemed reckless. Twenty million dollars was easily enough money to take my company to the next level, and the fact that someone had toggled that kind of money underneath my nose made me burn with anger. Ross wanted me to branch out and involve as many people as possible, but that didn't make sense to me either. More people knowing what was going on meant more of a chance it could get leaked to the media with a storm of bad press ensuing.

And that wasn't going to be good, either.

I didn't know what to do. I knew I could trust Markus's opinion, even if our needs for a situation didn't line up. I wanted to talk to him about security teams. Private detectives. I wanted to know what my best bet was going forward that didn't involve me going to the police.

They already knew Nina had tried to burn down my damn files room. They didn't need to know anymore.

I picked up the phone and called Markus. I knew he would help me out in a situation like this. He always had, no matter what type of advice I was asking him about. But his line kept ringing. I gave it a few minutes and tried him again, but it still shot me to voice mail. I decided to place a call to his secretary back in Alberta to see if she could get in touch with him, but all she could tell me was that he was in a few emergency meetings with his company.

Which I understood, given the reason he'd made his trip to Miami in the first place.

I drew in a deep breath before I reached over to my intercom. I pressed the button that led straight into Ross's office and asked him to come in when he had a moment. He was the only other person I trusted to volley these types of ideas against. I needed someone who didn't mind playing devil's advocate so I could make sure I was making the best decision for my company.

"You rang?" Ross asked.

"Can you come in and shut the door?"

"Shit. What the hell else has happened?" he asked as he shut the door.

"I know you and Markus have differing opinions on this, but I want to get your feedback on hiring a private detective," I said.

"You know I think you should involve the police," he said.

"And Markus thinks I should do close to nothing, yes."

"Is it a good move to have Markus know something this personal about our company?"

"I trust Markus with my life. It was the efforts he put in here for the first three or four years of Big Steps' life that put us where we are today. Up until he moved his own headquarters to Canada, he was a massive player with us. Without the risks he coached us into taking, we'd have none of this. So yes, I trust him with something like this."

"You don't have to get all defensive, but finances are finances, and even married couples sink with them sometimes. I don't want us making any hasty moves," he said.

"Like involving the police?" I asked.

"That's not a hasty move. Someone's stealing from us, Jimmy."

"And reallocating assets and all sorts of stuff. I've spent days digesting Ashley's notes and findings."

"Should we get her in here for this?" he asked.

"She called out sick today. Migraine."

"Again? Hasn't she been doing that a lot lately?"

"You have a very accusatory tone to that question. You wanna try that again?"

"I'm not accusing her of anything. All I'm saying is, even for a corporate employee—"

"You were the one who sanctioned a laptop for her to use so she could remote in. What did you expect her to do? Work here Monday through Friday and remote in on the weekends?" I asked.

"Jimmy. Back off. You're already coming at this with wound up emotions. You'll get nowhere this way."

I drew in a deep breath and tried to calm my nerves. But honestly? They were fried. I raked my hands down my face and turned my chair to Ross. He was sitting in the chair across from my desk, his leg over his knee and his hands in his lap. Had it not been for his terrible habit of biting his lower lip when he got nervous, I would've said he looked too calm for a situation like the one we were in.

"You're right," I said. "I'm sorry."

"Are you ready for me to outline the reality to you?" Ross asked.

"Yes. Go."

"If the investors find out about this, we could lose everything. With the media scandal we just had, they would surely bail, no matter what types of figures Ashley could throw at them. She was our only saving grace this time around, but we have no safety net."

"Yet you want to involve the police?" I asked.

"Because if we don't and the investors find out, they're going to automatically assume it's us taking the money."

"Why? What would make them jump to that conclusion?"

"You're not the only one who's been digesting those balance sheets. The first three years of the company have those same weird reallocations and debits, but no initials are involved. The only logical assumption is that we were doing something. Remember, we didn't get username or password attachments to anything until our fourth or fifth year. The investors will draw conclusions of their own before the police can even lift a finger—because they will get involved at that point underneath investor pressure—and we're done. Screwed. Boiled in hot water because we didn't want to involve them before the investors figured it out."

"They haven't figured it out up until this point," I said. "There isn't enough of a natural flag to do anything."

"We went from no one knowing to four people knowing and panicking. It's only a matter of time," he said.

"Well, none of that is going to happen. I'm not losing my company over something like this. But in that scenario, Markus's idea of keeping it low-key doesn't work, either, which brings me back to the middle ground. What do you think about a private detective? Possibly a team?"

"Before we even get there, I want to ask something. And it's redundant, so bear with me, because it needs to be revisited. Are we sure this isn't Nina?"

"Why does this need to be revisited?" I asked.

"Because I got a call from our lawyer early this morning. Nina's been bailed out of jail until her trial."

"She what?" I asked. "This isn't on the news, is it?"

Because that would be a damn good reason for Ashley to call in sick.

"No, it's not. None of this is. I've kept on our PR department to make sure this stays out of the media."

"Oh," I said. "Well, good."

Maybe Ashley was sick after all.

"And routing back to your redundant question, Ashley said she chased that lead down. In fact, she told me it was the first one she tried, given all that's happened. There was nothing that linked back to her at all."

"I could try to give it a look-see, just for a second opinion," Ross said.

"If you want to, that's fine," I said.

"And as far as your private detective or whatever goes, I think it's a good idea. We need to involve someone who can help us figure out what the hell's going on. I have no idea why in the world Markus would advise you to do nothing."

"He didn't say 'do nothing.' He said, 'keep it as in-house as possible.' As in, don't let the media catch wind of it."

"Then he'll be on your side when we hire PIs who can sign an NDA and keep their mouths shut," he said.

"You look into Nina one last time, and I'll start research private investigators who could possibly help us out. I want to have one hired no later than tomorrow afternoon."

"Sounds good, but you better hire one quickly. Even as we speak, these problems are probably still occurring. The newest balance sheet comes out in a few days, and I'm sure it'll piss us off."

"Did you get that packet from IT on the IP addresses we asked for?"

"I'm expecting it before lunch today," he said.

"Send me a copy when you get it."

"Will do."

The day was long, and the IP document from our tech department didn't yield any other answers. From the garbled jargon they used, it seemed like someone was rerouting their IP addresses all over the damn country. They said it would take some time to dig into what was going on, and even then, our IT department didn't have anyone employed to look into this like we needed.

Which only fueled my desire to hire a professional who could keep quiet.

I locked everything away and turned my mind to Ashley. She had sent me a text message just after lunch with a picture of the prescription the doctor had written for her, a very high dose of migraine medication as well as something to help with nausea.

And it sparked a small fear in my chest.

I left work, hopped into my car, and made my driver stop at the flower shop as well as the deli. I picked up a beautiful bouquet of softly-scented flowers along with a quart of brothy vegetable soup. Even though I had seen the prescriptions, I still felt like Ashley was hiding something from me. That nausea medication kept scratching at my mind, and her sudden onset of such a severe migraine had me worried.

Was it possible Ashley was pregnant?

I told my driver to park in the garage and wait for me. I had a feeling Ashley wouldn't want me to stay, and I didn't want to put her in a position where she felt the need to offer. I took the elevator up to her floor and knocked on her door, listening as she shuffled behind it.

When she opened the door, she seemed relatively all right.

"I take it the medication's working?" I asked.

"Are those for me?" she asked.

"Of course, they are. The soup as well," I said.

"Jimmy, you're so kind. Come on. I'll get them in some water."

I watched her walk and noted how stable she was on her feet. Minus the bags underneath her eyes and the light slump in her shoulders, she didn't seem to be sick. That could've been the medication hard at work, but it didn't do anything to abate the fears in my mind.

"I really wish you would've let me come with you this afternoon," I said.

"No offense, but your car is loud. It practically roars down the road," Ashley said.

"Is a cab quieter?"

"Immensely. It doesn't have a souped-up engine," she said. "No pun intended."

Her eyes dropped to the soup I was carrying before a grin crawled across her cheeks.

"Well, whatever the doctor has you on, it seems to be working," I said.

"It is. The medicine for the nausea was in case it was coming from a different source. But when I took the migraine medication, the nausea disappeared about an hour after the migraine did."

"I'm glad to hear it," I said.

"Are you staying for soup?"

"No. This all for you. I didn't want to crowd you if you were still unwell once I arrived. My driver's down in the garage."

"Are you upset I chose not to come into work?" she asked.

"I was the one who gave you the day. I'm glad you took it. It seems to have done you some good."

Her smile lit up her cheeks, and I couldn't help the way my eyes danced down her body. She took the flowers and the soup from me and quickly arranged the flowers in a vase she had filled. My eyes kept dropping to her stomach. Was it possible she could still be pregnant? Had the doctor run any kind of test like that? Was that something I should ask her?

My eyes whipped up to hers as she turned to me, a mug of soup in her hands.

"I've only seen people on television drink soup that way," I said.

"I eat cereal and milk from a cup too. Makes drinking the milk after easier," Ashley said.

"In another lifetime, you were probably an inventor."

"Or a connoisseur of pizza. I've eaten it so much in my lifetime that it only makes sense."

The two of us shared a little laugh before I walked over to her. I wrapped my arm around her, pulled her close, and kissed the top of her head. She was warm, welcoming, and inviting, instinctively curling into me like she always did. I closed my eyes and envisioned what she would be like pregnant with her stomach round with child and her breasts full. Heat shoot up my spine as I let her go, my eyes raking along the curves that would grow if she was pregnant, the thighs that would thicken and the hips that would widen.

Holy hell, Ashley would be beautiful pregnant.

"I hope you enjoy the soup," I said as I cleared my throat.

"Are you sure you don't want to stay?" she asked.

"If I do stay, I won't be able to contain myself."

"What do you mean?" she asked.

"Because even when you're sick, you're still the most beautiful woman I've ever laid eyes on."

Her cheeks flushed, and I felt my legs go numb. The things this woman did to me with a simple smile were unimaginable. I bent down and pressed a kiss to her cheek, chancing one last intimate encounter before I took my leave.

But I couldn't stop that question from running through my mind.

Was Ashley pregnant? And if she was, why wasn't she telling me?

Chapter 20

Ashley

What Jimmy had done for me was so sweet, but I was scared he thought I was lying to him. I could tell he was uneasy in my apartment yesterday despite his outward demeanor. I had already admitted to lying to him once about calling out sick, and I was concerned he didn't trust me. It was why I had sent him the prescriptions the doctor had written me in the office.

I went past Jimmy's office and decided to stick my head in. I opened the door and smiled, watching as his head whipped up from his papers. Instead of offering me a kind smile, his stern expression set in.

"You should knock," he said.

"I've never knocked before," I said.

"Well, you should. What if I had been in a meeting?"

Furrowing my brow, I closed his office door. Maybe he was simply having a bad morning. I walked into my office and kept my door open, hoping to get a peak of Jimmy whenever he left. But he stayed in his office all day and not once did he open his door so we could see one another.

He always kept his door open so we could see one another.

Shit, he thought I was lying to him about something. That had to be it. I saw him smile at his receptionist and have a friendly conversation with Ross. He hadn't ducked his head in to ask me if I wanted anything for lunch or even to offer having lunch in my office like he usually did.

Something was wrong, and I needed to talk with him.

"Ashley."

"Jimmy. Hey. I was just coming to find you," I said.

"Did you forget about the meeting this afternoon?" he asked.

"What meeting?" I asked.

"I put it on your calendar four hours ago."

"You never put anything on my calendar. You always come and tell me personally."

"Didn't have the time today. Come on. You've made us late."

I gathered up my things as tears welled in my eyes. I tried to blink them back as we flipped into a company-wide financial meeting. I took minutes of the meeting and recorded it, jotting down everything I could remember and making tick marks when I couldn't get everything down. The meeting was almost two hours long, and Jimmy didn't look at me once.

It was like he was intentionally trying to avoid me.

"Hey, Ashley. We're all going out for a bite to eat," Ross said. "Wanna come?"

I looked over at Jimmy, and he cleared his throat.

"Yes, Ashley. You should join us," he said.

Robotically, like it was required of him to invite me.

"Sure," I said. "I worked through lunch again, so I could go for a bite to eat."

"Stop doing that," Jimmy said. "You'll get this company in trouble if we get audited."

"Don't worry. I'm still clocking out for lunch," I said.

A bunch of us went out for lunch together, but Ross kept tossing us odd looks. Jimmy wasn't sitting next to me, and he rarely addressed me over the course of our meal. He didn't offer to pay, and he left before I could ask him to talk with me. Ross offered me a ride back to the company.

The car ride was silent, though I knew he wanted to ask questions.

The only bet I had was catching him after work. I sat in my office and tried to wrap things up. Then, I sent him an email with the minutes of the meeting in it. I stood from my desk as I saw his door rip open, and I ran up to him and grabbed his arm.

"Can we talk?" I asked.

"I've got a meeting with Markus," Jimmy said.

"I thought Markus was already gone?"

"He's extended his time in Miami. We're going for some drinks."

"That sounds like fun. Do you want some company?"

"I'll have Markus."

"I mean, Jamie might like some company," I said.

"She'll be fine."

His words punched me in the gut as I dropped my gaze to my feet.

"Call me later? Let me know how it goes?" I asked. "If you can."

"If I've got time, I will, Ashley."

"And be careful. Don't, you know, drink too many drinks and drive."

"My driver's taking me. I'll be fine," he said.

I watched him walk toward the elevator as Ross stuck his head out of his office. I didn't try to conceal the tears flooding down my cheek. I turned and headed for my office, determined to bury myself in some paperwork.

I called Cass and told her to pick up Chipper for me, so I knew he would be okay for the night.

"Ashley, what's going on?"

"Nothing. Just lots of work," I said.

"You've been crying," she said.

"No, I haven't."

"You're my best friend. I know when you've been crying. Did that asshole do something to you?"

"Jimmy? He's not an asshole."

"He is if he made you cry," she said.

I sighed and sat back into my chair as I turned toward the windows. Nighttime was descending onto Miami, and the town was coming to life. Jimmy was out to drinks with Markus and Jamie, and he was probably talking about how I was a liar, a filthy, bullshit liar like the rest of the women in his life were.

Or something like that.

"Ashley? You there?" Cass asked.

"I think I know who L.R. is," I said.

"What?"

"In fact, I'm almost positive I know who it is. The problem is it's someone this company trusts immensely, and I'm not sure Jimmy's going to believe me."

"Who the fuck cares? You have to tell him, Ashley. Why the hell have you not already told him?"

"So many reasons," I said.

"I don't know what the hell's going on in your mind or what happened at work today, but if you know who that person is, you have to tell Jimmy. Not Jimmy, your boyfriend. But Jimmy, your boss."

"What if he doesn't believe me?"

"Then that's on him. When have you ever given him the notion you couldn't be trusted."

I sighed as I closed my eyes.

"Ashley, what did you do?" she asked.

"I may have called in sick a time or two when I wasn't sick to work out who L.R. was and then told Jimmy I wasn't actually sick."

"Seriously, Ashley."

"I thought I was doing him a favor! Helping him, Cass. And now he doesn't trust me. I don't think, anyway."

"Why don't you think?" she asked.

"He's been acting strangely. I had to go to the doctor yesterday because of a bad migraine."

"And he thinks you weren't actually sick."

"I sent him a picture of the prescriptions I received. Hell, I could go get a doctor's note."

"But that kind of shit doesn't translate into 'I think I know who's stealing from you, but you won't trust me because I took a personal day once.'"

"I lied about the reason I took that personal day," I said.

"Apples to oranges. I'm telling you, Ashley. You have to tell him. How he reacts is on him. But you have to tell him what you know, even if you're flat-out wrong, because the alternative is you're right and his company goes under for it."

"I know," I said. "I know."

"Will you come get Chipper tonight? Or is he staying with me?"

"I'll come get him in a couple of hours," I said.

"We'll be waiting. Tell him, Ashley. Write him a note if you can't do it in person. But for fuck's sake, tell the man."

"I hear you, damn it. Okay? Sheesh."

"See you soon."

"Yep."

I hung up the phone and sat in my office for two hours waiting for Jimmy to call. I left my office and went to pick up Chipper and waited for him to call. I curled up with Chipper in my bed and listened to his soft snores as I watched the clock tick over to one in the morning.

I waited for a call that never came.

And it broke my heart.

Chapter 21

Jimmy

A knock came at my door, and I groaned. The last thing I wanted to do with my Friday morning was interact with anyone. Markus and I had indulged in way too much alcohol the night before, and I was fighting off a terrible hangover. I told him about Ashley. About how she had lied to me and how I thought she was still lying. Markus gave me some decent advice, which all centered around the fact that I had to come clean with her. I couldn't keep holding her at arm's length until she spilled the beans to me.

I had to tip the can and spill the beans myself.

"Come in," I said.

I heard the door open as a pair of soft footsteps padded in. I looked up and saw Ashley entering my office, her hair hanging down past her shoulders. She had her contacts in today, and her skin looked like it was glowing. I had a hard time ripping my eyes away from her in the dress she had worn to work. Her heels flexed her calves, and the soft fabric draped along her curves.

I sat up at my desk as my eyes traveled to hers.

"What's wrong?" Ashley asked.

I furrowed my brow as she took another step forward.

"Why have you been treating me like a pariah?" she asked.

I slid my chair back from my desk and walked around to perch on the edge of it. Her brazen demeanor was shocking, to say the least. Ashley was always so quiet and timid. But with her power dress on and her hair down and her vision free of her glasses, it was like I was staring at a new woman, a powerful woman.

It was alluring.

But it also meant her hormones were raging.

"I'm not going to ask you again, Jimmy," she said. "What's wrong?"

"Nothing's wrong," I said.

"That's a lie, and you know it. Yesterday, you didn't want to be around me, and you didn't call me after you were done with Markus last night."

"I don't answer to you," I said plainly.

"That. Right there. That tone of voice you take with every employee you can't stand. You've never taken that tone with me, and I haven't done anything professionally to deserve that tone."

"You've lied to me and taken sick days when you weren't sick. You know personal days aren't paid, so you took advantage."

"That's what this is about?" she asked. "You think I was trying to swindle you out of money?"

I was growing more and more worried as her gaze grew hotter. She was angry. Very angry. Angrier than I'd ever seen her before. Ashley wasn't an angry person. She was the most patient person I knew. My eyes fell to her stomach quickly before finding her eyes again, and I envisioned having a child with her. How her body would morph and how people in the office would look at her. How her hormones would rage like this and how she would start craving random things in the middle of the night. I'd have to move her in. Go to her doctor's appointments.

The mere idea of it all tugged a grin across my cheeks.

I wouldn't mind having a child with Ashley. With her intelligence and my looks and her beautiful eyes and my persistent demeanor, we would have an unstoppable force on our hands. I would have someone to pass my company down to, someone I trusted in this climate of people I couldn't trust.

"I know something's wrong, and I'm not leaving until you tell me what it is," Ashley said.

"Oh, I don't doubt it for a second," I said.

"Jimmy, we need to go—"

BUILDING BILLIONS - PART 2

Ross's eyes fell on Ashley, and even he was taken aback by what she looked like. Ashley's eyes swung to Ross, and I could see the worry that crossed his face. Her anger was apparent to someone more than me, which gave me relief.

I wasn't reading into things any more than anyone else would.

"What?" Ashley asked.

"Some of the investors are here," Ross said. "They wanna see you and Ashley."

"Why are they here?" Ashley asked.

"They've caught wind of our issues," Ross said.

In an instant, Ashley took off for the door. She left me in her dust as she shoved Ross out of the way. He shot me a look, and I shrugged him off, trying to tell him to let it go. She was hormonal, that much was for sure, and I didn't know if it was wise to have her in a meeting like this. But there was nothing I could do about it until after this meeting, and my only hope was that Ashley kept it together long enough to get through this damn thing.

Ashley was already fielding questions as I sat down at the end of the table. They were demanding to see the numbers, and she was trying to push back, trying to keep everything concealed despite her anger toward me.

I stood from my seat and cleared my throat to catch their attention.

"Ashley, it's okay. Show them the documents," I said.

"For the record, it's not any of their business," Ashley said. "The only accounts they need to be concerned with are theirs."

Then she got up from her chair and went into her office to get the information.

"As you can see, the transactions go back a long way, but none of them come from the investors' accounts," Ashley said.

"But you're telling me twenty million dollars has been funneled out from underneath the nose of this company?" Mr. Matthews asked.

"Over a long period of time, yes," she said.

"Do you have any idea who this L.R. person is?"

I watched Ashley tense as she threw her gaze over to me. There was something about her eyes that changed. The anger in them almost completely subsided, and in its place rose a worry that flipped my stomach. My mind began to swirl again as she drew in a deep breath. She needed to stop looking at me. She needed to hold her ground and answer their questions.

It was what I'd hired her for, and the last thing we needed was to look like she was being prompted.

"We have some theories, but nothing concrete yet. It was why we hadn't stepped forward with this information yet," Ashley said.

Theories? We had theories?

What the fuck was this woman hiding from me now?

"And when were you going to tell us about this?" Mr. Matthews asked.

"When we knew who L.R. was and had them in custody," she said. "Because this does not affect investor's accounts, it is none of your concern."

"I beg to differ," Mr. Matthews said.

"Then someone else should. Most of your checks have bounced before they cleared, so if any investor should be upset, it's certainly not you."

"Then I'll ask," another investor said. "What happens financially at this company is for us to look into."

"So long as it affects the money you give and the profits you reap. Everything else is out of your jurisdiction," Ashley said.

"Then how about this for jurisdiction? This company has until the end of the week to get to the bottom of whatever this is in these balance sheets. If you don't, we walk."

"All of us," Mr. Matthews said.

"I can assure you, we will get to the bottom of it," I said.

Ross escorted them out of the room, and I shot a look over to Ashley. If she couldn't reign in these pregnancy hormones of hers, then she was going to lose her damn job. She couldn't come at the investors with that kind of attitude, especially when we had no grounds to stand on in terms of who the fuck L.R. was.

And now, we had until the end of the week because of her big ass mouth.

"My company's done if they walk," I said.

"You can find more investors," Ashley said.

"It's not that simple," Ross said.

"Then you better do whatever you're going to do to figure out who L.R. is," she said.

"Something tells me you have a theory," I said.

"Would you believe me if I told you?" she asked.

"I don't know what's going on with the two of you, but it stops now. You can resume the couple quarrel once we stop this ship from sinking," Ross said.

"Fine," I said. "But we start investigating now. Ross, there's a number to the private detective agency I enjoyed the most on my desk. Call them, and tell them I'll double their initial offer if they can get here within the hour and get to work."

"Got it," Ross said.

"And Ashley?"

"What?" she asked.

"Take some deep breaths. We'll get through this. I'm not leaving you alone in this. I trust you, whether you think I do or not."

I watched her body relax, and it all but confirmed my suspicions. She was pregnant. Why she was making me dig it out of her, I had no idea. But I wasn't leaving her during this time. She was obviously scared, and the stress from this entire situation was getting to her, but no matter what, she wasn't doing this alone.

She had me whether she wanted me or not.

Chapter 22

Ashley

I pulled up to Cass's apartment and started for her door. I needed to talk to my best friend. I didn't need a lecture, and I didn't need her telling me what to do. I needed a decent, extremely biased conversation. I needed her to be in my corner to try and sympathize with me. I clutched the two coffees I held in my hands as I reached my foot out, knocking my toe against her door.

She whipped it open and cooed at Chipper before she took a coffee from my hand.

"Did we have a date I forgot about?"

"No," I said. "But I do need something from you."

"What's up?" Cass asked.

"I need my best friend."

"You've got me," she said.

"No. I need my biased best friend, the one that's always in my corner, the one who's ready to bash heads in the second I start crying because she thinks someone's hurt me."

"Has someone hurt you?"

"Can you give that to me? Can you give me that person today?"

"Of course, I can. What's going on, Ashley?"

"Things with Jimmy are falling apart."

"Did you tell him what you knew?" she asked.

"No, I haven't yet."

"Why the hell not? You have to."

"No, I can't. You don't get it. He's already upset with me over fuck-knows-what. He's been acting weird and pushing me away, and I'm not sure what to do about it."

"The first thing you need to do is tell him about—"

"I'm not here to talk about work!"

Cass jumped back as tears rose to my eyes. Why couldn't she do this for me? My life was falling apart, and I still had to go see my mother, and I was trying to raise my spirits. I wanted someone to tell me Jimmy was being an asshole, that none of this was my fault, he was being a dick, and that I had nothing to worry about. I didn't want to talk about work or L.R. or who I thought it was. I didn't want to talk about Markus or our conversation or even fathom how Jimmy would react once I told him my theory.

"Okay. I'm sorry. Um, what's going on with you and Jimmy?" Cass asked.

"I think he's upset that I even found the error in the first place."

"I thought we weren't talking about work," she said.

"As long as you don't tell me to tell him shit, we'll be okay," I said.

"Okay. As long as you know that's where my opinion lies."

"He's been pushing me away. A bunch of us went out to a late lunch yesterday after a financial meeting, and he didn't even sit next to me."

"Why not?" she asked.

"I don't know. I thought it was because he didn't trust me or something. You know, because of the sick days that weren't sick days. But then we had a meeting that went horribly wrong, and he looked at me and told me to take a few deep breaths. He said we would find a way out of this and that he trusted me. Looked me right in my eyes and said it."

"So what's the issue?"

"Why has he been avoiding me if he trusts me?" I asked.

"Is he still avoiding you?"

"Yeah. I called Jimmy this morning to see if he wanted to do dinner tonight. You know, to talk about that thing."

"Good. What did he say?"

"He turned me down. Said he was going golfing with Markus and to dinner with him after and that we could meet up tomorrow," I said.

"So you meet him tomorrow."

"You don't get it. When Markus first got to town, Jimmy couldn't get me out with him enough. Every time they got together, he wanted me there. The night before last, they went out for drinks. Markus's girlfriend went, but Jimmy didn't invite me. I even offered to keep him company, and he said no."

"Why?" she asked.

"I don't know, Cass. I really don't. I told him to call me if he could whenever he got home and was safe, but his call never came. I stayed up until one thirty waiting for it."

"Fuck him, then. If this isn't a trust issue, then he's got no reason to treat you this way. And even if he did have trust issues, he needs to be a damn adult and talk to you about it instead of acting like a fucking toddler."

"Thanks, Cass."

"No, I'm fucking serious. Ashley, if he's doing things like this to you and pushing you away, then I'd be concerned that this Markus asshole is saying something about you in his ear."

"But Markus likes me," I said. "He wouldn't do that. Right?"

"This Markus guy a businessman?"

"Yeah. He's Jimmy's mentor."

"Then his opinion means a lot to Jimmy. He's talking about you. Jimmy's got something up his ass, and instead of talking to you about it, he's dancing around you."

"How do I get him to talk to me?" I asked.

"Corner him. Ask him point blank what's wrong."

"I did that already. The meeting interrupted us yesterday."

"Then do it again and again until he finally comes clean. You said the two of you were getting together tomorrow, right?"

"If he doesn't cancel, yeah."

"Then do it tomorrow. Corner his ass and man up. Then grow some balls, woman up, and tell him what you need to tell him," she said.

"I knew you were gonna slip that in there somewhere."

"I held out as long as I could. You'll be okay, Ashley. I know you like this guy but dating in the workplace is hard. And if this all goes south, you'll have me."

"Thanks, Cass."

"Got any plans for your day?"

"I'm going to see my mom. They've approved Chipper coming if I meet Mom outside, so I'm gonna introduce her to the newest addition to my family," I said.

"I think she'll like that. If anything, she'll like the fact that your dad hated dogs."

"That's what I'm banking on."

I hugged Cass's neck and set off for the nursing home. I tried to shove Jimmy to the back of my mind as I parked my car. This was time spent with my mother. This wasn't time for him to be ruining. I had to let go of whatever was going on between us and be there for my mother. She was rocking on the porch with a nurse at her side, and she looked like she was having a good day.

I drew in a deep breath before I picked up Chipper and got out of my car.

"That my Ashley I see?" my mother asked.

"And Chipper," I said.

"You brought a rat to see me?" she asked.

"It's a beagle puppy," I said. "His name's Chipper."

"Your father hated dogs."

"Which was why I got one."

"I like the way you think," she said with a grin.

"How are you feeling today?"

"I'm doing all right. Slept until nine this morning."

"That's late for you. Stay up late partying?" I asked.

I set Chipper in my mom's lap, and a small smile crept across her cheeks.

"A game of pinochle got a little rowdy last night," my mother said.

"Sounds like a good story. What happened?" I asked.

"I don't wanna waste my time talking about some card game. I want you to tell me how your new job is going."

I was shocked she remembered and felt my spirits lifting even more.

"It's going well. We've hit some snags, but that's corporate life. I got moved into a new place, and I love it, thanks to my fun new paycheck."

"I noticed my account had more money in it than I recalled," she said.

"Consider it an early birthday present."

"I don't know what I'm going to spend it on. I never go anywhere," she said.

"Then go somewhere now. Take one of those trips with the pinochle gang and treat them to lunch. I'm sure they would love that. And you might too."

"It's been a while since I've enjoyed something like that. I just might."

"I think you should," I said.

The two of us sat there, rocking in chairs on the porch of the nursing home. She was stroking Chipper, and he was falling asleep in her lap. I took in the sun on my face and the comfort it brought to be sitting there, talking with my mother.

Then, I heard her rocking chair stop.

"Mom?" I asked.

"What's this dog doing in my lap?" she asked.

I looked up at the nurse before she gathered Chipper off my mother.

"Whose dog was that?"

"I'm sorry. He's mine," I said.

My mother's gaze whipped over to me, and I could tell she didn't recognize me.

"Who are you? Why am I outside?"

"I came to visit. We're sitting outside for it," I said.

"I never gave my permission to come outside. That's how it works, right? You have to have my permission?"

"Why don't we get you inside, Mrs. Ternbeau?" the nurse asked.

"Who is this woman? Why am I out here with her?" my mother asked.

I stood from the rocking chair as tears rose to my eyes.

"I think I should go," I said.

"What in the world is happening? Why would you put me out here with a stranger? I don't feel safe here anymore. Get me out of here. Call my daughter. Tell her to come get me!"

I clutched Chipper close to me as I made my way to my car. Tears were welling in my eyes as I ducked down into my car. I watched the nurse walk my mother inside, her voice getting louder with each complaint. She was demanding they call me even though I was sitting right there. She was telling them she didn't feel safe there any longer if they were willing to sit her out on the porch with a stranger.

She wanted me to come and fix it, but she couldn't even recognize me.

I settled Chipper in the passenger's seat as my phone rang. Someone from inside the nursing home was calling, and I debated whether to pick it up. I knew my mother was in good hands. I knew they were doing the best for her that they could. I had the strongest urge to call Jimmy, but I knew he would be angry with me.

Interrupting his guy time or whatever with Markus.

"Hello?" I asked.

"Ashley, I'm so sorry," the nurse said.

"It's okay. She was lucid there for a little while, and that's all that matters," I said.

"I wanted you to know that the nurse has her calm. She's about to sit down and eat lunch."

"Thanks for calling. Take care of her, okay?" I asked.

"I know you don't always agree with what we do in the moment, but she is loved here."

"I know she is. It's hard to watch her constantly bucking against people and having to be poked with needles. I hate needles, and I know she hates them too."

I heaved a heavy sigh as I leaned my forehead against the steering wheel.

"Thank you for everything you do for my mother," I said.

"That's what we're here for. But she's settled and eating lunch, and I figured you might want to know," the nurse said.

"Thanks. If she asks about me again, tell her I love her, and I'll be by soon."

"We always do because we know you'll make good on your word. You'd be surprised the number of people we have here who don't have family visit them ever."

"Well, that'll never be my mother, okay?" I asked.

"We know. For what it's worth, when she does talk about you, her face lights up."

A tear streamed down my cheek as I drew in a shaky breath.

"I'll talk to you guys soon," I said.

"Talk to you soon," the nurse said.

Chapter 23

Jimmy

I drove to Ashley's apartment and waited for her downstairs. She came out in a pair of pants and a shirt with her body wrapped in a cardigan. I furrowed my brow as she looked around, not spotting me sitting at the curb in the car waiting for her. She was dressed like we were going fishing, not like I was taking her out to lunch.

Was she not feeling well again?

"Ashley."

I rolled down the window, and her eyes met mine.

"Hey. I didn't think you'd be driving," she said. "You usually make me come down when you're not driving."

"There wasn't any guest parking in the garage. Come on. Let's go get some food," I said.

She climbed into the car but kept her arms crossed over her body. She was closed off, and her body was pushed against the door. I wanted to make conversation with her, but the air between us was tense.

I didn't like it.

I wanted to find a way to alleviate it.

"Drinks with Markus went well. I'm sorry I didn't call. I didn't get back in until almost three," I said.

"I'm glad you had fun," Ashley said.

"He asked a lot about you."

"I hope he's doing well."

"Jamie wasn't with him tonight. She wasn't feeling well so she decided to stay in."

"I'm sorry to hear that," she said.

"You probably would've been bored anyway."

"Not really. I enjoy hanging out with Markus."

I drew in a deep breath as I settled my eyes on the road. I drove out just past the town city limits to this small place I knew about. She wasn't dressed to go where I originally wanted to take her, so I figured somewhere quiet and low-key would help her. I didn't know if it was her migraine or her morning sickness that was doing it, but either way, she would be comfortable. This place had wonderful soups and breads she could munch on and all sorts of flavored waters.

I could have them put some ginger in it for her stomach.

I escorted her into the restaurant, but she wouldn't let me take her hand. She kept moving it away from mine and stepping away from my hand on her lower back. She usually leaned into my touch, walked beside me and tucked herself underneath my arm. But today was different.

It was like she was trying to get away.

"How're you feeling today?" I asked.

"Okay. Had a rough visit with my mom yesterday," Ashley said.

"How so? Is she okay?"

"You know, lucid one moment and not lucid the next. She met Chipper and loved him until she didn't recognize us."

"Why didn't you call me? I could've come and helped."

"I did. Earlier that day. You told me you were going to be with Markus all day."

"I would've left for something like that."

"Would you have?" she asked.

Her eyes flashed with anger for a moment before our waiter came to take our order. Ashley ordered some soup with some buttered bread and a fresh glass of strawberry and ginger water. I studied her and the way she was caved in on herself. There were bags under her eyes. The lackluster way she was looking around told me Ashley wasn't sleeping well, probably because of the morning sickness.

But her picking at her food did me in.

Instead of eating her soup, she swirled it around, watched the broth make patterns with the vegetables as she sipped her water. Why was she doing this? Why was she prolonging telling me? What did she think was going to happen? Did she think I was going to abandon her, cast her off to the side? I loved her. Sure, we were hitting a rough patch, but couples did all the time.

Why did that translate to hiding her pregnancy from me?

"Do you not like the soup?" I asked

"It's good soup. I'm just not very hungry."

"You could've told me that. We could've gone and done something else," I said.

"It's not a problem. I'll eat it in a second."

"Are you feeling okay, Ashley? You've been off the past few days."

"I could say the same about you," she said.

"What do you mean?"

"Asking me to knock when I come into your office. Keeping your door closed so we can't see one another. Sitting away from me at lunch after that meeting. Hell, putting that meeting on my calendar instead of coming to tell me yourself. You used to look for any excuse to come see me. Why has that changed?"

"You're upset because I'm treating you like an employee?" I asked.

"No. I'm upset because I know that's a lie."

"Then you know how it feels," I said.

"I told you, I took those days to try and figure out what was going on with those balance sheets. The first one I took was simply because I didn't have them finished, and I needed to get them finished."

"So there was more than one."

Ashley bit down on her lip and shook her head. She leaned back in her chair, away from me as her eyes gazed out the window. She was breathing deeply, and her neck was flushing red.

"You've been getting very upset recently and very easily, I might add."

"Maybe because you won't tell me why you're all of a sudden avoiding me like a pariah," she said.

"Because I know you've been stressed about something. And yes, it might partially be because you took sick days and lied to me about them. I'm supposed to be able to trust you."

"You told me you trusted me Friday. Are you saying you lied to me then?" she asked.

"Would you have a leg to stand on if I was?"

"Yes, because what I was lying to you about was helping me figure out this mess your company is in. You lying to me about something personal like that is a completely different ballgame."

I wanted to tell her it wasn't. I wanted to tell her she was lying by withholding this pregnancy from me, but I wanted us to have a nice afternoon. I wanted to create an environment where she felt she could talk to me about this, and the tension and anger we were throwing at one another wasn't helping.

"I'm sorry if I've been distant," I said. "The stress of this issue at the company is getting to me. A lot."

"You're not the only one," Ashley said softly.

"I get it. I do. And I'm sorry I've been taking it out on you. I'm frustrated that I've been given a deadline by the investors, and I'm frustrated they found out in the first place. I'm frustrated that the private detective agency hasn't found anything, and I'm just coming out of my skin with frustration."

"I get it," she said.

Her eyes met mine, and I saw all the hurt in the galaxy behind them. Her eyes were watering with tears, and my heart ached for her. I got up from my chair, walked around the table, and offered my hand to her. I didn't want to make her move if she didn't want to. I didn't want to jostle her and make her sick.

But the moment she took my hand, I pulled her to my body.

"Why don't we go back to my place and watch a movie, huh? Wind down, release a bit of stress, and just be with one another before the week starts?"

"I've missed you," Ashley said breathlessly.

"I'm right here," I said.

We got our food and drinks to go, and we headed back to my place. Ashley had unfurled from her body, and she was letting me hold her hand. I felt like things were slowly settling down between us. She wasn't pressed against the door, and I even caught her staring at me a time or two.

I smiled at her whenever I caught her eye and watched that beautiful blush tint her cheeks.

We walked hand-in-hand up to my penthouse, and the first thing she did was head for the bathroom. I stood there close to the door, listening to see if I could hear any puking sounds. Heaving sounds. Muffled groans. Anything to give me a leg to stand on when I brought this up. But I didn't hear anything, and I went to go put our food away so she could finish up whatever she was doing.

"Jimmy? Where'd you go?"

I closed my eyes as I put everything in the fridge.

"In the kitchen," I said. "Would you like a glass of wine?"

"I'm not really in the mood for wine. Did you take my water back there?" she asked.

That was enough for me. Ashley had never turned down wine in my presence.

Ever.

"Jimmy? What's wrong?"

I turned to Ashley as I nodded my head to the cup on the edge of the counter.

"That's your water," I said.

"Thanks."

"Why are you hiding this from me?" I asked.

"Hiding what?"

"Come on, Ashley. Stop it. I know what's going on. I know what you're still hiding from me."

"Wait, what?" she asked.

"Why don't you trust me with this? What do you think's going to happen? What? You think I'm just gonna cast you out or something?" I asked.

"Yeah, actually. I'm pretty scared of losing my job over it."

"Why would I fire you over something like this?" I asked. "Not only could I get sued for something like that, but I care for you. I wouldn't fire you over something like this. We'd find a way to get around it."

"Get around what? There isn't anything to get around, Jimmy. It's happening, whether you want it to or not."

"And I get that, Ashley."

"You're insane," she said. "You don't get anything."

"I know your hormones are a little out of whack right now, but what we need to do is get you to an actual doctor who can help us with this," I said.

"What?" she asked.

"Why am I having to dig this information out of you in the first place? I know why you went to the doctor, Ashley. And you don't have to worry. We can figure out how to work a baby into our life."

I watched confusion wash over her face as she set her water down. She cocked her hip out as her eyes darted around my face. I stood there, waiting for her to confirm it, waiting for her to finally show me the beans I had already spilled. If she wasn't going to tell me, then I was going to tell her I knew. She wasn't as secretive about this as she thought, and the longer she stared at me, the angrier I got.

"Just say it, Ashley."

"You think I'm pregnant?" she asked.

"Aren't you?"

"No."

"Stop lying. I know you are."

"No, Jimmy. I'm really not. And the fact you think I would keep something like this from you if I were pregnant is telling me you don't really know me at all."

"I didn't think you would call in sick when you weren't sick, but that happened twice," I said.

"Jimmy, you either forgive me for those or you don't. But you don't get to continue to tell me you're fine with it and then bring it up in an argument when it suits you. And no, I'm not fucking pregnant."

"I know you are. The nausea medication. The mood swings. The pale skin. The picking around at your food. The migraines. Turning down wine. Ashley, that's your go-to drink. You never turn down wine."

"And you were never ashamed of being seen with me until this past week. You didn't want to stand by me, interact with me, sit with me at lunch, or anything else for that matter. You didn't even bother to call me to let me know you were okay after drinks with Markus."

"You said if I could, to call you. I couldn't call you. I was drunk."

"Then send a damn text message, Jimmy! For fuck's sake, I was up until almost one thirty waiting to make sure you were okay!"

"See? Mood swings," I said.

"Because you're an asshole, not because I'm pregnant!"

"Stop lying to me. I don't do that in a relationship. At all," I said.

Ashley began laughing as she turned her back to me.

"You really think I would keep something like a child from you," she said.

"I don't really know what to think right now," I said.

"I think you've got bigger problems than fighting with me about some imaginary pregnancy. Jimmy, I've been on the pill for years. I take it like clockwork. I'd have to come off that thing for months before I could even think about getting pregnant. We are not pregnant. Nowhere near it."

"Bigger problems?" I asked. "And what would those be?"

"The fact that you can't see what's right in front of your nose, Jimmy! Your company is tanking, and you won't do anything to save it because you're too wrapped up in—"

I felt my own anger boiling my blood as Ashley stopped what she was saying.

"Go ahead. Say it," I said.

"This isn't the time or the place," she said.

"Say it, Ashley."

"No."

"Stop holding things back from me and say it. This is my company, and if you have information about what's going on, I need to know what it is!"

I watched her eyes grow wide as I settled myself down on my feet. She was two seconds away from bolting out the door. I had yelled so loud at her, my ears were ringing. My throat was hurting, and my hands were balled into fists. What the hell was going on? How had this spiraled so far out of control? Ashley grabbed her water and started down the hallway, and I strode after her to keep her from leaving.

"Where are you going?"

"Home," she said.

"What about our movie?"

"Fuck your movie," she said.

She went to open the door, but I closed it with my hand. She tried to open it again, grunting with all her might.

"Let me out," Ashley said.

"Not until you talk to me."

"You lost that right the moment you yelled at me. Now let me out of this apartment."

"All I'm asking you to do is let me in. Talk to me. Stop hiding things from me. You don't have to protect me, and you don't have to shut me out. All you have to do is be honest with me."

"You want honesty? Fine. I'll give you honesty. You won't protect your own company. Instead of following the advice of your best friend and business partner, you let some investor who comes into town once a year make the decision for you. Now, the investors know what's going on, and they're threatening to tear everything down, all because you keep leaning on Markus. Markus this and Markus that and Markus is the holy grail of everything. Well, what if he's not?" she asked.

She looked up at me as my hand slid away from the door.

"What if he's not?" Ashley asked.

"What do you know?" I asked.

"You can make an appointment with me for tomorrow," she said.

"You tell me what you know right now."

"What I know is you have nobody to blame for this but yourself. Your company's tanking, and instead of helping with the investigation, you're fighting me over some fantasy pregnancy."

"Would that not be important? If you had been pregnant, would that not have been worth my time?"

She opened the door as tears streamed down her cheeks. She stepped out into the hallway, clutching her water tightly in her hand. My mind was racing, and at the same time, it was standing still. It felt like I was sinking to the bottom of an endless ocean, farther and farther away from the people I cared about. The people I loved. People like Ross and Markus and my receptionist.

People like Ashley.

Just ... Ashley.

"Why are you lying to me?" I asked. "What do you get from keeping this from me?"

She snickered and shook her head before she drew in a deep breath.

"You're fighting the wrong battle, Jimmy."

"I'm fighting the one I need to fight," I said.

"Leave me alone," she said. "I don't know what in the world has gotten into you, and I don't care. Just go away."

I watched her walk down the hallway, making her way to the elevator. She pressed the button and leaned heavily against it, her forehead pressed into the wall. My heart was breaking. I was more confused than ever. I got no straight answers from her except what she really thought about me.

And what was that she didn't care.

Her head leaned into the wall, and her shoulders began to shake. I wanted to go to her and find a way to comfort her during this time together. But I knew she needed space, and I knew she needed time. We were going through a lot, and the company was on its last leg, and the last thing I needed was to push Ashley away too.

I couldn't lose her, not when I needed her the most.

But then, I saw it. I watched her heave in the hallway. Her shoulders shook with her muffled sobs as she covered her mouth, and then it happened again.

Her stomach lurched, and she held it back.

She stepped into the elevator, and I ran after her. I tried to get there in time, but it was fruitless. The doors shut on her before I could press the button, and I heard the elevator carrying her down the floors.

I looked over to the stairs and rushed down them. I took every single step two-by-two, trying to beat the elevator down. I prayed it stopped. I prayed I had enough time to get to her. I prayed the elevator got held up by someone getting on at a different floor so I could meet her at the bottom.

She was sick, and she was heaving. She had to be pregnant.

I was sweating down the back of my shirt as I ran down all twenty-three flights of steps. I busted out into the main lobby, my eyes darting around for her. I heard the elevator doors open, and I turned, waiting to swoop her up in my arms and carry her right back upstairs.

But instead, an older man with a much younger woman got off.

I ran outside, looking around to see if I could see her, see a cab carrying her off, or see her walking down the sidewalk. But the more I looked, the less I saw. The longer I spent trying to spot her, the more time she had to get away from me like she wanted.

I raked my hand through my hair as I walked around in circles. I couldn't go back up to my penthouse, but I couldn't go to her. What the hell was I going to do? Was Ashley really not pregnant? And if she wasn't pregnant, then why was she heaving at the elevator? Was she really that upset?

Had I upset her that much?

I started for the only place I knew, the only place that had given me solace for the past twelve years and the place I was about to lose if my detective team couldn't figure out what the hell was going on with the discrepancies.

I walked down to the parking garage, got in my car, and went to work.

Chapter 24

Ashley

"Ugh, this coffee is always so good," I said.

"The clock is ticking," Cass said.

"Holy hell, would you get off it? I'm talking to him today about it," I said.

"Good. I want you to let me know how it goes."

"Hardly. You've been riding my butt about this, and I'm tired of hearing you chirp in my ear."

"Until you can woman up and chirp in your own ear, I'm always going to be there to do it for you."

"I don't think he'll believe me, especially after the fight we had over the weekend."

"Whoa, whoa, whoa. Back up. What fight?" she asked.

"We had lunch yesterday, and it spawned a huge fight between us. He knew I was hiding something from him, and I told him that wasn't the time or the place to talk about it. But do you know what he accused me of hiding?"

"What?" she asked.

"Being pregnant."

"He what?"

"Yeah. He told me to stop lying to him and admit that I was pregnant. We've all been on edge this week with everything going on, and I admit, I've been bouncing between my emotions pretty strongly. One minute I'm anxious and the next I'm upset. But I told him I wasn't pregnant, and he unleashed."

"What do you mean by unleashed?"

"Apparently, he's still upset that I used a couple of sick days without being sick."

"No, he's upset because you told him you were sick when you weren't."

"Isn't that what I said?" I asked.

"No, it's not. But as long as you agree that's the issue, I won't break it down for you," she said.

"I told him I wasn't pregnant, and he told me to stop lying to him. I told him he had bigger issues on the table than me being pregnant with some child that didn't exist. Then, we said a lot of things we didn't mean."

"Like?"

"I told him he was idly standing by while his company tanked."

"You what?" she asked.

"And he told me he didn't know what to think about me anymore because he couldn't trust me."

"That's ... not a terrible reaction given the scenario."

"Then we laid out everything, how he's been treating me lately and how my mood swings have been bad. My skin's apparently paler and me not eating my lunch translated into morning sickness somehow."

"Are you pregnant?" she asked.

"Hell, no, I'm not pregnant. I am worn down and worried about all this stuff with the company. But Jimmy lied to me, too. He looked me in my eyes on Friday and told me he trusted me, point blank in front of Ross. Less than two days later, he's telling me he doesn't and he doesn't know what to believe because he doesn't know if I'm telling the truth."

"You two need a break. You need to put this shit at the company behind you, sit down together, and have an adult conversation. But you can't do that until this issue's resolved."

"Which is why I'm talking to him today about it," I said.

I finished my coffee and hugged Cass before I went to work. I headed straight for Jimmy's office, ready to receive whatever punishment was going to come my way.

But when I knocked on his door and jiggled the doorknob, I found his office locked.

Furrowing my brow, I dug out my cell phone. Jimmy was never late for work. Was something wrong? I dialed his cell, but it shot me straight to voice message.

Great. He was screening his calls.

"He's not coming in for the day."

I turned around and took in the receptionist sitting at her desk.

"Is he sick?" I asked.

"No. Just called in and said he was taking a personal day," she said.

"Did he say where he was? I've got something very important to discuss with him."

"All he said was to hold all of his calls and meetings until tomorrow," she said.

I sighed as I looked down the hallway to Ross's office. He would know where Jimmy was. I walked down the hallway, darted into the office, and waited patiently for Ross to look up at me.

"I can feel you standing there, Ashley."

"Waiting for you to finish," I said.

"What's up?" he asked.

"Do you know where Jimmy is today?"

"No. He called in and said he needed a personal day but didn't give any specifics. Why?"

"I needed to talk to him today about something."

"Is it something you can talk to me about?" he asked.

"You might want to be there, but it needs to be with Jimmy around," I said.

"Well, he'll be back in tomorrow. We can catch him then."

Instead of heading for my desk, I headed for the elevator. Jimmy wasn't getting out of this that easily. Just because he pissed me off didn't mean I called in for a personal day. And now that I needed to talk to him about something important, he was doing the one thing he didn't like of me.

I mean, it was sort of like what I had done.

Fuck. It was all so confusing.

I rode down to the parking garage and started up my car. I raced to his apartment and parked at the curb. If there was anywhere he would be during a time like this, it was in the comfort of his apartment. I placed a quarter in the meter and ran up the steps, busting into the main lobby.

I didn't stop for anyone calling my name as I made my way to the elevator.

I rode it up all the way to the penthouse level. The doors opened, and I darted down the hallway to Jimmy's front door. I rose my fist and banged on the heavy wooden surface, not intending to stop until I heard his footsteps.

But the longer I banged, the more my fist hurt.

I took my cell phone out and dialed his number again. I was listening for the ringing before he ignored my phone call again. It rang out twice, and I pressed my ear to the door to see if I could hear it. His voice message picked up again.

However, there was no ringing coming from inside his apartment.

I leaned my forehead against the door and groaned. Where the hell was Jimmy? I needed to talk with him. It was important, and this wasn't the kind of information to relay to him through Ross. What kind of businessman didn't come to work during the most important week of his company's life?

What was wrong with him?

Chapter 25

Jimmy

Taking a day off work helped me to try and sort through some things. The private detective agency was keeping me abreast of their findings, but it didn't look good. It was taking them longer than they thought to trace all the IP addresses, and they would be cutting things close. I told them to use whatever they needed, and I would shovel the difference out-of-pocket. I needed this wrapped up by the end of the week.

I couldn't stand to lose any of my investors.

I drove myself out to the beach and rented a condo for the night. I was still confused and hurt by Ashley and what had happened between us. I knew, now more than ever, that she was pregnant. The heaving by the elevator confirmed it for me. Why she was still hiding this from me, I had no idea, and it felt like a knife was piercing my gut. After everything we had been through with Nina and what we were going through with her mother, all I wanted was the truth from her.

And she couldn't even give it to me.

I came into work early, hoping to avoid her. This week was important, and I needed all the space I could get to figure things out. I was pouring over documents that had long since been buried in the files room to see if I could find any leads. I was trying to bat away the investors who were now bugging Ashley, Ross, and me. I felt my world crashing in around me, and I still couldn't concentrate.

Not with Ashley's office just down the way.

A soft knock came at my door, and I felt my gut turn over on itself. I knew who was out there. I knew who was knocking on my door. Ross had informed me that she had been looking for me all day. The front lobby told me she had come in yesterday morning in a trance trying to find me. Maybe she was ready to talk, ready to finally admit to me what was going on with her so we could get her to a doctor and get her through this.

Though with her mood swings, she would probably have to take a backseat in the company. Because they were getting bad.

"Come in," I said.

"Could we talk?" Ashley asked.

"Shut the door behind you and take a seat," I said.

I watched her walk across the room, and I could see the fear in her body language. The way she hid behind her glasses. The way her hair spilled in her face. The way her shoulders were slightly caved in as she sat. She was petrified, and I didn't know why. I had no clue what I had done to make her think I would be upset over something like this.

I was ready to put this behind us, save my company, and move forward with our family.

"Are you ready to admit it?" I asked.

"Yeah, but I'm still not pregnant," she said.

"Come on, Ashley. Stop with the—"

I watched her dig around in her purse before she pulled out a bag full of pregnancy tests. She tossed it onto my desk and kept her purse on her lap, her eyes boring into my face.

I picked up the bag, looked at the tests, and all of them were negative.

"Can we get on with it now?" Ashley asked.

"You're not pregnant," I said.

"Nope."

"But you didn't eat lunch."

"Because I wasn't hungry, Jimmy."

"And you were heaving at the elevator."

"I was sobbing at the elevator. What you saw was my trying to hold back sobs," she said.

"You were you crying that hard?"

I felt my stomach drop to my toes as Ashley's face hardened.

"Yes," she said.

"But you've been on edge, and your skin is paler. I know you see it. It's obvious you haven't been getting much sleep," I said.

"Thank you for pointing out how shitty I look," she said. "But we've all been on edge with everything going on in the company."

"But you've had it the worst," I said.

"Because I know who L.R. is."

The bag dropped from my hands and to my desk as I sat forward.

"What?"

"It took me a little while to piece everything together, but I know who it is. I've been in a rough state because I've been trying to figure out how to tell you, but I know you won't believe me, not after this fight over trust," she said.

"Ashley, how long have you known this?" I asked.

"Since Saturday," she said.

"Okay. Who is it?"

"Remember when we went to get drinks with Markus? You know, the time Jamie couldn't make it?"

"Uh, yeah. I do. Why?" I asked.

"Markus and I had a long discussion while you were in the bathroom about our mothers."

"Ashley, stop beating around the bush."

"Sit back and listen, Jimmy. It's for your own good."

I clenched my jaw as I sat back in my chair.

"Markus and I talked about our mothers and how they both struggled with Alzheimer's. He mentioned his mother calling him Lou one time. He said something about it being his father's name, and he thought maybe she thought he was his dad or something. Then, he told me another story about how there were times when, like my mother, she would forget she had been married. His mother would correct the nurses whenever they called her Bryant. She would tell them her last name was Roth, not Bryant."

I felt the breath leaving my lungs as I took in Ashley's every word.

"If you combine 'Lou' and 'Roth' together, you get the initials L.R. You also said Markus has been here since the inception of the company, guiding you and giving you advice. Did you ever give him control of the finances at some point?" she asked.

"Of course, I did. Because I trust Markus. What are you saying, Ashley?"

"When did Markus leave to establish his headquarters in Alberta?" she asked.

"What the fuck does that have to do with anything?" I asked.

"Was it three years into the establishment of your company?"

"Markus is not the one behind this. Without that man, we wouldn't be here right now."

"Of course, he would want to help you. He's siphoning money from you. He said he was here because of company issues, and I looked up some things. There are articles being run about him, rumors going around that his company is struggling financially. Has he talked about it at all?"

"Shut up," I said.

"Jimmy, I know you want to trust him. I can't imagine how hard this is for you to hear, but you have to believe me. Everything about his story makes sense and fits. Why he's staying in town longer. Why the initials didn't exist on any of the balance sheets until three years in. Jimmy, he even reacted strangely when we clued him in on what was going on. How defensive he—"

"I said, shut up, Ashley!"

I flew up from my chair and slammed my hands on my desk. Was this woman insane? Did she really think Markus, of all people, would be behind something like this?

"Jimmy, I said you wouldn't believe me, but it doesn't change the fact that it's true," she said.

"You're crazy," I said.

"I'm not. You're upset, and I get it. But this is happening. This is serious."

"It's not true," I said. "Markus would never do anything like that to me."

"Jimmy, take a deep breath and think about this logically."

"You want me to think logically? After your emotional tirades over the past few days? Accusing me of being ashamed of you and pushing you away? I introduced you to the only man I ever considered to be a father to me. I met your mother and went along with her degraded state so I could cultivate a relationship with you. I promoted you, secured you a career that could give you everything you could've ever wanted. I made you comfortable, and I pulled you into my life and bent over backward to make you happy, and this is how you repay me?"

I watched Ashley stand from her seat and take a few steps away from me.

"It's pretty shitty of you to be so upset with me, you would try to put the blame of something like this on someone so close to me, someone you know I love and respect with everything I have."

"That doesn't change what he's doing, Jimmy. Just because you love him doesn't mean he's not doing this," she said.

"You can't stand it, can you?"

"What?" she asked.

"You can't stand not being the center of attention in my life. You've been jealous ever since Markus came into town."

"What? No. I liked Markus until I figured out what he was doing to you."

"Where's your proof?"

"I just gave it to you."

"That isn't proof. It's some stories you laced together, stories Markus trusted you with that you're now twisting to use against him like Nina twisted shit to use against me."

Ashley continued to back up toward the door as I came around my desk.

"In this moment, you're no better than her. You've taken stories an innocent man trusted you with, and you're throwing them back at him spitefully because you can't stand that someone else has my attention."

"Jimmy, that's not what—"

"I should've seen it the moment you got upset with me for not calling you after going out drinking with him Friday night. One night with me and him. Just one. You attended all of the others, but you couldn't stand one night!"

"Jimmy, you've got this all—"

"Get out," I said.

I watched her open the door as she stumbled out of my office.

"Get to work."

The last thing I saw were tears welling in her eyes as I shut the door in her face. I couldn't believe it. After falling in love with her, she turned around and showed her true colors. I would have to tell Ross what she was doing in case she went behind my back like Nina did to try and take my company down. I raked my hands through my hair and yelled out into my office, filling the corners of the room with my anger.

Fuck.

Chapter 26

Ashley

"You did the right thing," Cass said.

"I told you he wouldn't believe me," I said.

"He had to know. Despite how he reacted, he had to know the truth."

"I'm not crazy, right?"

"No. Now that you've explained it, it makes perfect sense. Now, because of his stubbornness, he'll lose his company over it."

"He doesn't deserve that."

"And you don't deserve the way he talked to you," she said.

I laid in bed with Cass at my side. I didn't go to work, nor did I call in. I didn't care to be there any longer. I didn't care what happened with Big Steps. I was still reeling from how Jimmy talked to me, the anger in his eyes and the aggressiveness of his actions.

"He said I was the same as Nina," I said breathlessly.

"Listen, you're nothing like that bitch. This falls on his shoulders now. You did your part and washed your hands of all this," Cass said.

"I can't be with someone who talks to me like that," I said.

"I agree with you, but is that what you want? To break up with him?"

"It is. But I want to do it face-to-face."

"No text message breakups here?" she asked.

"No. I want to look him in his eyes before I walk away from him. I want him to know this was all because of him. We allowed the stress of Nina and his company and this entire situation get in the way of something beautiful."

"Do you love him?"

I felt tears brewing at the back of my eyes, but I refused to cry. I wasn't going to shed any more tears over this man. I had cried enough, and it was time for me to move on, even if it meant leaving the company altogether.

"I think I could have," I said. "Given enough time. I do care about him, but I don't know if we can come back from this. I don't know if I'll ever feel safe around him again."

"Do you want me to go with you when you break up with him?" Cass asked. "I could sit in the car or something."

"No. I need to do this on my own. I need to start being able to make these moves without people pushing me to do it. We've run our course, and who knows? Maybe I've run my course with Big Steps in general."

"That's a serious step, Ashley. You'd have to find a job and quickly. You can't afford this apartment otherwise."

"I'll figure it out along the way. I'll make sure my mother's taken care of, and I'll make sure I have a roof over my head. I always do. It's not fair the way he treated me, and I know it'll affect our working relationship from here on out."

"If there's a company after the end of this week," she said. "When are you going to do it?"

"I'm going to call him and see if he can get drinks with me tonight. I'll do it then."

"Want me to stick around here? For when you get back?"

"Will you?" I asked.

"Of course, I will, Ashley."

I reached over and grabbed my phone. I sighed as I dialed Jimmy's number and held the phone to my ear. I was honestly shocked he picked up, but I could tell he wasn't happy it was me.

"Ashley."

"Hey, Jimmy. Listen, are you free tonight?" I asked.

"Why aren't you at work?"

"For the same reason you weren't yesterday," I said.

"You should've called in if you wanted a personal day."

"Well, I'm calling now. We need to talk," I said.

There was a silence on the other end of the line before I heard Jimmy shuffling around.

"What time and where?" he asked.

"Seven? There's a place near my apartment called—"

"Seven at The Shack. Got it. See you then."

Then he hung up on me, and I tossed my phone across the room.

Cass stayed with me for the rest of the day before I headed out to meet Jimmy. I knew this wasn't going to end well, but it needed to end. Whether it cost me my job or not, I wasn't sure we could ever come back from this. My hands were shaking as I walked into the bar, and I scanned the room to see if Jimmy was there yet.

And when I didn't see him, I headed for a booth in the back.

I was sipping on a glass of wine when he sat down in front of me. His eyes were cold, and his face was stern. He was still in his business suit, and he was distant.

I knew then and there I was making the right decision.

Because he had already shut me out.

"Thanks for meeting me," I said.

"Thanks for finally calling in," Jimmy said.

"Do you want anything to drink?"

"I've already got something coming. I'm ready whenever you are."

"How are things going with the detectives?" I asked.

"You mean have they found anything to support your insane claims?" he asked.

I drew in a deep breath as I cast my gaze out the window. I wasn't going to let him get to me. I wasn't going to let him intimidate me like he could other people.

"I'm ready for your apology whenever you're ready to give it," Jimmy said.

"Apology?" I asked. "For what?"

"Isn't that why we're here? So you can apologize for barging into my office and claiming my mentor's behind all this?"

I gawked at Jimmy as I turned my gaze back to him.

"You thought I brought you out here to apologize?" I asked.

"Only logical explanation," he said.

"No, it's your logical explanation based on your out-of-control emotional demeanor, but I didn't ask you to drinks to apologize."

"Well, it certainly isn't a date," he said.

"No, it's not. Because we aren't together."

I watched the life drain from behind Jimmy's eyes as his posture faltered.

"What?" he asked.

"I told you the truth yesterday about Markus and the proof I had. Whether you choose to believe it or not is on you. If you don't believe, you'll lose your company. It's that simple, but I'm done here."

I watched him clench his jaw as he straightened back up.

"With us," Jimmy said.

"Yes. With us. After watching you morph into … whatever it was you were yesterday, I could never feel safe with you again. I don't think you will ever trust me again, and I know I'll never trust you enough to come to you with anything. Nothing important, anyway. I have a feeling this will undoubtedly affect our working relationship, but I'll focus on that another day."

Jimmy's eyes locked onto mine, but he didn't pipe up with anything of his own. I drank down the rest of my wine, pulled out my wallet, and threw a fifty-dollar bill on the table.

"To cover you and me," I said.

I scooted away from the booth and turned my back on Jimmy. He didn't come after me, and he didn't call out my name. He didn't try to stop me nor did he run up behind me. I walked out of the bar and stood at the curb, allowing the cold air to dry the tears threatening to spill over my cheeks.

A part of me still wanted him to come after me, but I knew he wouldn't. I was nothing more than a thorn in his side, a "Nina" he needed to get rid of. I wondered if this was how the breakup between them went down, if he left her or if she got fed up and left him. I ran across the road, taking the only opening I had as I reached the sidewalk on the far side of the road.

I turned back to see if I could see him, to see if he'd thought about things and decided to come looking for me.

But he wasn't coming out of the bar, and he wasn't standing on the edge of the road. He wasn't calling out my name or asking me to come back. I stood there for a few minutes and finally watched him emerge, and my heart soared.

Maybe he was coming to find me.

Maybe he was going to cross the street and come to my apartment.

But instead, he flagged down a cab and got in. He disappeared into the dark, dank atmosphere, and the cab drove off down the road, leaving me standing there as I pined over a man who didn't deserve me.

He didn't care, and it was obvious what I had to do, even if it was going to make things difficult for a while.

Chapter 27

Jimmy

I sat in the living room all night staring out the window. She left. Ashley had left me. My secret weapon for my company and the woman I had given my heart to had shattered it at her feet. I sipped bourbon all night as I turned her words around in my head. As much as I hated to admit it, Ashley at least appeared right. The pieces did fall into place, even though I didn't want them to. My only other course of action was to talk to Markus myself. The detective agency wasn't getting anywhere, and I was tired of them floundering around with no answers.

So I decided to get them myself.

"You wanted to see me?" Markus asked.

"Yes," I said. "I want to talk to you about something."

"Holy shit. You look like hell. You and Ashley stay up late last night?" he asked.

"There are some things that have been brought to my attention about this ... financial debacle," I said.

"Did your detective agency finally find something?" he asked.

"No. It was a talk I had with Ashley."

I leaned against my desk as I looked into Markus's eyes.

Was that uncertainty I saw?

"What's she got to do with any of this?" Markus asked.

"Why so defensive?"

"Not defensive. Just wondering what her place in all this is," he said.

"She said the two of you talked about your mothers."

"Did I offend her or something?"

"No. Not really, but there were a couple of stories you told her that led her to believe L.R. stands for 'Lou Roth.'"

"And you believe her?" he asked.

"Not really sure. My gut reaction says no, but the look in your eyes makes me wonder if I took the wrong side," I said.

"The look in my eye. You now some expert on body language?"

"I learned from the best," I said with a grin. "Is it true your company is struggling financially?"

"Where the hell did you hear that?" he asked.

"A couple of articles I found last night."

"You look like you've been drinking. You sure you didn't hallucinate all this?"

"Yeah, I'm sure. I saved them on my phone in case you wanted to see them. There are rumors circulating that your company's been struggling financially for a while now. Is that why you're in town?"

"I told you I had to sort out some shit with my company, Jimmy."

"And why have you extended your time here?" I asked.

"Because my company's fucking struggling. What the hell's this got to do with anything? Why the fuck did you call me in here?"

"Why so agitated?" I asked.

"Because you're wasting my time."

"I looked through the balance sheets this morning and came across something I'd forgotten. Ashley mentioned to me that the first three years of balance sheets had all these transactions, but no initials attached to them."

"So what?" Markus asked.

"You left Miami three years into my company being established so you could build your new headquarters in Alberta. I placed a call to a trustworthy contractor of mine and asked him for a rough estimate of how much that building might've cost you."

"What? I don't—What the hell's this gotta do with anything, Jimmy? Get to the point."

"I am," I said. "That contractor said your headquarters would've cost you around four million to build."

"That building's worth a hell of a lot more than that."

"It is, with all the bells and whistles you added later. But the shell of the building is around four million, so I tallied up some things."

I held Markus's gaze as he began to shift his weight on his feet. Holy fuck, this confident man I had entrusted all of my business practices to was losing his footing.

Was Ashley right about this? Had I just fucked everything up?

"Are you curious to know what I found?" I asked.

"No," Markus said.

"Over the first three years of this company, four million and change was siphoned from underneath my fucking nose."

I watched Markus bite down on the inside of his cheek.

Ross came into the office and alerted me that it was time for the investor meeting. I stared Markus down as my heart thundered in my chest. Ashley had been right. She'd been right this entire time, and I was too blind to see it. I escorted Markus into the meeting, not letting him out of my sight. I told Ross to go get the detectives before we started the meeting, and then I took my seat at the head of the table.

"We waiting for something?" Mr. Matthews asked.

"We are. Give me five minutes," I said.

The detectives slipped into the room, and Markus started to sweat. Visibly sweat. I locked my eyes on him as Ross took a seat, and I could tell he was quickly putting the pieces together.

"I know who's been stealing from this company," I said.

"Then it's about time you inform us," an investor said.

"Markus Bryant," I said.

"Jimmy, maybe we should talk outside?" Ross asked.

"Don't worry. That mentality already cost me one person I care about. I'm not going to let it tank my company as well," I said.

"This man's reckless," Markus said. "He's flailing and grasping at straws because his company's about to go under with scandal. First, the social media issue and now this."

"I trusted you," I said. "I looked up to you as if you were my own father, but I can't deny what's so plainly in front of my nose."

"Do you have any proof?" Mr. Matthews asked.

"Yes, do you have proof?" Markus asked.

"Only the entire conversation Markus and I just had in my office. Would you like me to plug my phone in and play it for everyone? Or do you want to give up now and see what kind of deal your lawyers can cut you?" I asked.

Everyone slowly turned their gaze to Markus. Every single shark investor I had at that table was boring their eyes into his skull. I watched his eyes pan around the room as he stumbled over his words, trying to defend himself and talk his way out of the corner he had been backed into. This man, who was confident and crass and unashamed of his power, was stumbling over his words and sweating down the back of his neck.

"I've been making payments back into the accounts," Markus said.

"Holy hell," Mr. Matthews said.

"I know you see those credits. I've seen the balance sheets. There aren't simply withdrawals, Jimmy. There are credits too," Markus said.

"There are. Three million dollars against the twenty million you've siphoned off Big Steps for twelve years," I said.

"Detectives, arrest that man," Ross said.

"I was going to pay back the rest of the money once my company becomes profitable again. We've been struggling. Jimmy, I know you know what it's like to struggle financially. Come on. Just think of it as a loan. You aren't struggling financially. You can afford to lend me this money," Markus said.

I watched the detectives slap handcuffs on Markus. They hauled him out of the room as all the investors watched. I didn't know what to think. My heart was broken, my soul was empty, and the only person I would've leaned on during something like this wasn't at work.

Why wasn't she at work? She should've been here for this. She'd earned her right to gloat.

"Well, Mr. Sheldon, it looks like you've found your culprit," Mr. Matthews said.

"Ross can take this meeting from here. I kept Miss Ternbeau at a distance once she came to me with the information she had pieced together. It's time for me to call her and tell her this is finished," I said.

I pushed away from the table and got up as Ross took my place. He started fielding questions from the investors and doing his best to get everything back on track. I strode to my office, slamming my door, and reached for my phone.

I had to call Ashley and talk to her.

I dialed her cell number, but it shot me to her voice mail. I dialed again, and I got the same response. I hung up my office phone, pulled out my cell phone, and dialed her number again.

But she still wasn't picking up.

She hadn't been to work for two solid days. No explanation, no call to my receptionist, and no call to Ross. I had to get her back. I had to get her back in my life and in the life of this company. Once this mess got cleaned up for good, I was going to take this company to heights it had never seen, and I wanted her at my side professionally and personally.

I was ready to grovel, to get on my knees and beg for her forgiveness. I was prepared to pay her any salary she wanted and bend to any will she had for us so long as she could come back.

I went to pick up my office phone and dial her again, but a flash on my computer screen caught my eye.

I had an email.

And it was from her.

I held my breath and clicked the link to open it. My gut warned me that something was about to drop.

Mr. Sheldon,

While I have enjoyed working for Big Steps, I can no longer work my job in good faith to the best of my ability. I wish you the best in your future endeavors, whatever they may bring.

Ashley Ternbeau

I read the simple email over and over again. I sent her one back, begging her to come in and talk to me, to meet me for drinks. Or food. Or on the beach for a walk. Or at my apartment. Or at her apartment. I told her she was right. It was Markus who'd siphoned money from the company and that I was sorry for ever doubting her. I apologized for ever getting as angry as I did with her and all of the fighting we had been doing while the stress at the company had been mounting.

I told her I would take her anywhere, agree to any terms, and talk on any ground as long as she would talk to me.

Then I sent the email off into the ether before I flopped down in my chair.

I had nothing else I could do. She wasn't picking up my calls, and I had a feeling she wouldn't answer my email. She wasn't coming back to work, but I refused to process her termination papers. I'd cash in her paid vacation. Her medical vacation. Her personal days. I would max out every ounce of leave I could give her before I would process her leave from this company.

My world was collapsing around me, and I needed her to help me get it back on track. I just needed her.

THE END

Part 3

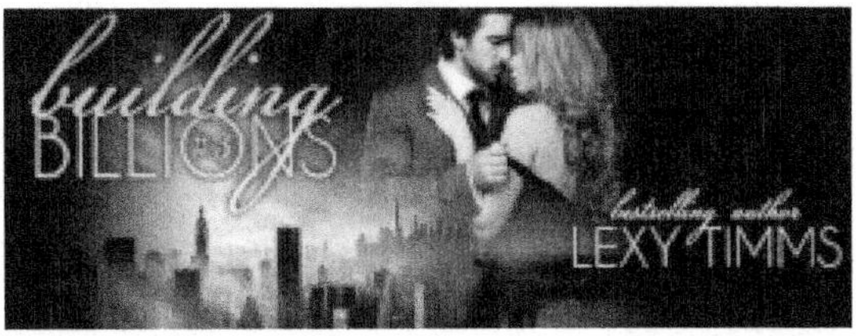
building
BILLIONS
bestselling author
LEXY TIMMS

Part 3 Blurb:

Building Billions

Part 1
Part 2
Part 3

Find Lexy Timms:

LEXY TIMMS NEWSLETTER:
http://eepurl.com/9i0vD
Lexy Timms Facebook Page:
https://www.facebook.com/SavingForever
Lexy Timms Website:
http://www.lexytimms.com

Want

FREE READS?

Sign up for Lexy Timms' newsletter
And she'll send you
A paid read, for FREE!

Sign up for news and updates!
http://eepurl.com/9i0vD

More by Lexy Timms:

FROM BEST SELLING AUTHOR, Lexy Timms, comes a billionaire romance that'll make you swoon and fall in love all over again.

Jamie Connors has given up on men. Despite being smart, pretty, and just slightly overweight, she's a magnet for the kind of guys that don't stay around.

Her sister's wedding is at the foreground of the family's attention. Jamie would be find with it if her sister wasn't pressuring her to lose weight so she'll fit in the maid of honor dress, her mother would get off her case and her ex-boyfriend wasn't about to become her brother-in-law.

Determined to step out on her own, she accepts a PA position from billionaire Alex Reid. The job includes an apartment on his property and gets her out of living in her parent's basement.

Jamie has to balance her life and somehow figure out how to manage her billionaire boss, without falling in love with him.

** The Boss is book 1 in the Managing the Bosses series. All your questions won't be answered in the first book. It may end on a cliff hanger.

For mature audiences only. There are adult situations, but this is a love story, NOT erotica.

FRAGILE TOUCH

"HIS BODY IS PERFECT. He's got this face that isn't just heart-melting but actually kind of exotic..."

Lillian Warren's life is just how she's designed it. She has a high-paying job working with celebrities and the elite, teaching them how to better organize their lives. She's on her own, the days quiet, but she likes it that way. Especially since she's still figuring out how to live with her recent diagnosis of Crohn's disease. Her cats keep her company, and she's not the least bit lonely.

Fun-loving personal trainer, Cayden, thinks his neighbor is a killjoy. He's only seen her a few times, and the woman looks like she needs a drink or three. He knows how to party and decides to invite her to over—if he can find her. What better way to impress her than take care of her overgrown yard? She proceeds to thank him by throwing up in his painstakingly-trimmed-to-perfection bushes.

Something about the fragile, mysterious woman captivates him.

Something about this rough-on-the-outside bear of a man attracts Lily, despite her heart warning her to tread carefully.

Faking It Description:

HE GROANED. THIS WAS torture. Being trapped in a room with a beautiful woman was just about every man's fantasy, but he had to remember that this was just pretend.

Allyson Smith has crushed on her boss for years, but never dared to make a move. When she finds herself without a date to her brother's upcoming wedding, Allyson tells her family one innocent white lie: that she's been dating her boss. Unfortunately, her boss discovers her lie, and insists on posing as her boyfriend to escort her to the wedding.

Playboy billionaire Dane Prescott always has a new heiress on his arm, but he can't get his assistant Allyson out of his head. He's fought his attraction to her, until he gets caught up in her scheme of a fake relationship.

One passionate weekend with the boss has Allyson Smith questioning everything she believes in. Falling for a wealthy playboy like Dane is against the rules, but if she's just faking it what's the harm?

BUILDING BILLIONS - PART 2

Capturing Her Beauty

KAYLA REID HAS ALWAYS been into fashion and everything to do with it. Growing up wasn't easy for her. A bigger girl trying to squeeze into the fashion world is like trying to suck an entire gelatin mold through a straw; possible, but difficult.

She found herself an open door as a designer and jumped right in. Her designs always made the models smile. The colors, the fabrics, the styles. Never once did she dream of being on the other side of the lens. She got to watch her clothing strut around on others and that was good enough.

But who says you can't have a little fun when you're off the clock?

Sometimes trying on the latest fashions is just as good as making them. Kayla's hours in front of the mirror were a guilty pleasure.

A chance meeting with one of the company photographers may turn into more than just an impromptu photo shoot.

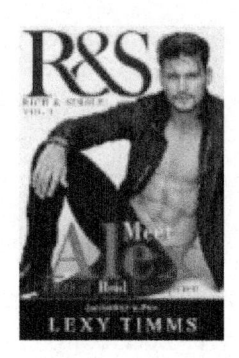

Hot n' Handsome, Rich & Single... how far are you willing to go?
MEET ALEX REID, CEO of Reid Enterprise. Billionaire extra ordinaire, chiseled to perfection, panty-melter and currently single.

Learn about Alex Reid before he began Managing the Bosses. Alex Reid sits down for an interview with R&S.

His life style is like his handsome looks: hard, fast, breath-taking and out to play ball. He's risky, charming and determined.

How close to the edge is Alex willing to go? Will he stop at nothing to get what he wants?

Alex Reid is book 1 in the R&S Rich and Single Series. Fall in love with these hot and steamy men; all single, successful, and searching for love.

Book One is FREE!
SOMETIMES THE HEART needs a different kind of saving... find out if Charity Thompson will find a way of saving forever in this hospital setting Best-Selling Romance by Lexy Timms

BUILDING BILLIONS - PART 2

Charity Thompson wants to save the world, one hospital at a time. Instead of finishing med school to become a doctor, she chooses a different path and raises money for hospitals – new wings, equipment, whatever they need. Except there is one hospital she would be happy to never set foot in again—her fathers. So of course he hires her to create a gala for his sixty-fifth birthday. Charity can't say no. Now she is working in the one place she doesn't want to be. Except she's attracted to Dr. Elijah Bennet, the handsome playboy chief.

Will she ever prove to her father that's she's more than a med school dropout? Or will her attraction to Elijah keep her from repairing the one thing she desperately wants to fix?

HEART OF THE BATTLE Series

In a world plagued with darkness, she would be his salvation.

No one gave Erik a choice as to whether he would fight or not. Duty to the crown belonged to him, his father's legacy remaining beyond the grave.

Taken by the beauty of the countryside surrounding her, Linzi would do anything to protect her father's land. Britain is under attack and Scotland is next. At a time she should be focused on suitors, the men of her country have gone to war and she's left to stand alone.

Love will become available, but will passion at the touch of the enemy unravel her strong hold first?

THE RECRUITING TRIP

Aspiring college athlete Aileen Nessa is finding the recruiting process beyond daunting. Being ranked #10 in the world for the 100m hurdles at the age of eighteen is not a fluke, even though she believes that one race, where everything clinked magically together, might be. American universities don't seem to think so. Letters are pouring in from all over the country.

As she faces the challenge of differentiating between a college's genuine commitment to her or just empty promises from talent-seeking coaches, Aileen heads to the University of Gatica, a Division One school, on a recruiting trip. Her best friend dares who to go just to see the cute guys on the school's brochure.

The university's athletic program boasts one of the top hurdlers in the country. Tyler Jensen is the school's NCAA champion in the hurdles and Jim Thorpe recipient for top defensive back in football. His incredible blue-green eyes, confident smile and rock hard six pack abs mess with Aileen's concentration.

His offer to take her under his wing, should she choose to come to Gatica, is a temping proposition that has her wondering if she might be with an angel or making a deal with the devil himself.

THE ONE YOU CAN'T FORGET

Emily Rose Dougherty is a good Catholic girl from mythical Walkerville, CT. She had somehow managed to get herself into a heap trouble with the law, all because an ex-boyfriend has decided to make things difficult.

Luke "Spade" Wade owns a Motorcycle repair shop and is the Road Captain for Hades' Spawn MC. He's shocked when he reads in the paper that his old high school flame has been arrested. She's always been the one he couldn't forget.

Will destiny let them find each other again? Or what happens in the past, best left for the history books?

** This is book 1 of the Hades' Spawn MC Series. All your questions may not be answered in the first book.

LEXY TIMMS
CONFESSION OF A
Tattooist
Lexy
Timms
Grab Your
FREE
Copy Today!

FORTUNE RIDERS MC
BILLIONAIRE BIKER
LEXY TIMMS
Download For
FREE
Lexy
Timms

Fire HOUSE ROMANCE
CAUGHT in FLAMES
BESTSELLING AUTHOR
LEXY TIMMS
LIMITED TIME
Lexy Timms
FREE
DOWNLOAD

ONE YOU CAN'T Forget
BESTSELLING AUTHOR
LEXY TIMMS
Lexy Timms
Grab Your
FREE
Copy Today!

Lexy
Timms
THE
BOSS
Managing the Bosses: Book 1
Lexy
Timms
Grab your
copy today!

FOREVER
FOREVER
FOREVER
BOOK 3
BOOK 2
BOOK 1
Saving
FOREVER
Lexy
Timms
for
99cents

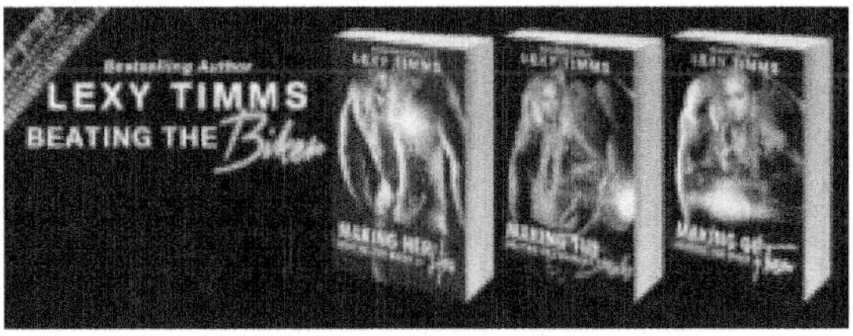
Bestselling Author
LEXY TIMMS
BEATING THE

LEXY TIMMS
MOMENT IN TIME: BOOK ONE
HIGHLANDERS
Bride

Don't miss out!

Click the button below and you can sign up to receive emails whenever Lexy Timms publishes a new book. There's no charge and no obligation.

https://books2read.com/r/B-A-NNL-BXCS

BOOKS 2 READ

Connecting independent readers to independent writers.

Did you love *Building Billions - Part 2*? Then you should read *Facade* by Lexy Timms!

The light at the end of the tunnel is not an illusion. The tunnel is.

I didn't become a billionaire sitting on the couch.

Sure, I come from money, but I turned that money into millions and billions more.

Somehow though, I've landed myself in hot water and someone wants my money, or me dead. Probably both. I hired a bodyguard from an agency that assured me they only work with the best.

Their best is a pretty, dark haired girl with an amazing body?

I'm screwed.

Royally.

Literally.

Screwed.

Billionaire in Disguise Series:

Facade
Illusion
Charade

Also by Lexy Timms

A Chance at Forever Series
Forever Perfect
Forever Desired
Forever Together

Alpha Bad Boy Motorcycle Club Triology
Alpha Biker
Alpha Revenge
Alpha Outlaw
Alpha Purpose

BBW Romance Series
Capturing Her Beauty
Pursuing Her Dreams
Tracing Her Curves

Beating the Biker Series
Making Her His

Making the Break
Making of Them

Billionaire Holiday Romance Series
Driving Home for Christmas
The Valentine Getaway
Cruising Love

Billionaire in Disguise Series
Facade
Illusion
Charade

Billionaire Secrets Series
The Secret
Freedom
Courage

Building Billions
Building Billions - Part 1
Building Billions - Part 2

Conquering Warrior Series
Ruthless

Diamond in the Rough Anthology
Billionaire Rock
Billionaire Rock - part 2

Dominating PA Series
Her Personal Assistant - Part 1
Her Personal Assistant Box Set

Fake Billionaire Series
Faking It
Temporary CEO
Caught in the Act
Never Tell A Lie
Fake Christmas

Firehouse Romance Series
Caught in Flames
Burning With Desire
Craving the Heat
Firehouse Romance Complete Collection

Fortune Riders MC Series
Billionaire Biker
Billionaire Ransom

Billionaire Misery

Fragile Series
Fragile Touch
Fragile Kiss
Fragile Love

Hades' Spawn Motorcycle Club
One You Can't Forget
One That Got Away
One That Came Back
One You Never Leave
One Christmas Night
Hades' Spawn MC Complete Series

Heart of Stone Series
The Protector
The Guardian
The Warrior

Heart of the Battle Series
Celtic Viking
Celtic Rune
Celtic Mann
Heart of the Battle Series Box Set

Heistdom Series
Master Thief

Just About Series
About Love
About Truth
About Forever

Love You Series
Love Life
Need Love
My Love

Managing the Bosses Series
The Boss
The Boss Too
Who's the Boss Now
Love the Boss
I Do the Boss
Wife to the Boss
Employed by the Boss
Brother to the Boss
Senior Advisor to the Boss
Forever the Boss
Gift for the Boss - Novella 3.5
Christmas With the Boss

Moment in Time
Highlander's Bride
Victorian Bride
Modern Day Bride
A Royal Bride
Forever the Bride

Outside the Octagon
Submit

Reverse Harem Series
Primals

RIP Series
Track the Ripper
Hunt the Ripper
Pursue the Ripper

R&S Rich and Single Series
Alex Reid
Parker

Saving Forever

Saving Forever - Part 1
Saving Forever - Part 2
Saving Forever - Part 3
Saving Forever - Part 4
Saving Forever - Part 5
Saving Forever - Part 6
Saving Forever Part 7
Saving Forever - Part 8
Saving Forever Boxset Books #1-3

Southern Romance Series
Little Love Affair
Siege of the Heart
Freedom Forever
Soldier's Fortune

Tattooist Series
Confession of a Tattooist
Surrender of a Tattooist
Heart of a Tattooist
Hopes & Dreams of a Tattooist

Tennessee Romance
Whisky Lullaby
Whisky Melody
Whisky Harmony

The Brush Of Love Series
Every Night
Every Day
Every Time
Every Way
Every Touch

The Debt
The Debt: Part 1 - Damn Horse
The Debt: Complete Collection

The University of Gatica Series
The Recruiting Trip
Faster
Higher
Stronger
Dominate
No Rush
University of Gatica - The Complete Series

T.N.T. Series
Troubled Nate Thomas - Part 1
Troubled Nate Thomas - Part 2
Troubled Nate Thomas - Part 3

Undercover Series
Perfect For Me
Perfect For You
Perfect For Us

Unknown Identity Series
Unknown
Unpublished
Unexposed
Unsure
Unwritten
Unknown Identity Box Set: Books #1-3

Unlucky Series
Unlucky in Love
UnWanted
UnLoved Forever

Standalone
Wash
Loving Charity
Summer Lovin'
Love & College
Billionaire Heart
First Love
Frisky and Fun Romance Box Collection

Managing the Bosses Box Set #1-3

Printed in Dunstable, United Kingdom